Riding the Waves

RIDING THE WAVES

An Erotic Anthology
by the
Houston Writers Guild Press

Edited by Elizabeth Ann Domino

Notice: *Some stories contain explicit scenes and sexual content. For discerning readers only.*

PRESS

RIDING THE WAVES
Copyright © 2016 Houston Writers Guild

Cover illustration by Paul Krumrei, Jr.
Interior design by David Welling

Houston Writers Guild Press
PO Box 42255
Houston TX 77242
www.houstonwritersguild.org

Ordering Information:
Quantity sales. Special discounts are available on quantity purchases by corporations, associations, and others. For details, contact the publisher at the address above.
Orders by U.S. trade bookstores and wholesalers. Please contact Houston Writers Guild Press at houstonwritersguild.org.

Printed in the United States of America

Publisher's Cataloging-in-Publication data
Riding the Waves / Houston Writers Guild
p. cm.
ISBN 978-0-9969824-2-9

First Edition

CONTENTS

⋙ FOREWORD ⋘

Elizabeth Ann Domino

AS MANY FRIENDS and family tell me, I cannot understand what it is to be a gay person in society today. And they are right. I can sympathize and empathize, but I will never understand being targeted with oppression, violence and discrimination based on who or how I love.

On June 26, 2015 in a landmark 5-4 ruling of the Supreme Court, I came a step closer to understanding this as I watched people I loved and cared for rejoicing in something I took for granted or brushed off as so menial.

So much so I failed once, and am working diligently at an attempt in number #2 . And still wonder if marriage is really for me.

When it came time to publish our second *Waves* anthology, it was unanimously decided that romance and erotica would be our next venture. Who doesn't love a good book riddled with sexual tension and impassioned couplings?

Entry after entry poured in, and as we began to read through submissions, we realized that we needed to publish two volumes instead of one. The overwhelming response included a majority of LGBTQ based romance/erotica, and we came to realize how underrepresented gay writers and stories were in our community.

Exploring this type of literature allows us to discover our hidden innermost sexual and carnal selves. These stories offer affirmation, vindication, fellowship, validation and a sense of shared identity that is needed now as much as ever within the gay community.

Offering an intimacy some may not otherwise be willing to share, we ask you to read these amazing tales with an open mind. And an open heart.

YOGIC YEARNINGS

Copper Hayes

IT WAS THE tiny blonde instructor: the one with the Tinkerbell. I lolled my head to watch her through slitted eyes as she settled onto her mat.

Her opening words—an invitation to recline in a comfortable position—had my legs splayed. That "letting go" of the world into the mindful stillness of yoga fluttered my labia open, and I kegeled. Tiny pulsing contractions.

Could she see the movements shudder my lips wider in my sprawl?

Her voice, strong enough to carry but soft and throaty enough to curl my toes, asked anyone who didn't want to be adjusted to cross both hands over their hearts.

"Thank you," she said to some fool who didn't want to be touched. She dipped her head toward the supplicant as if in benediction.

I deepened my breathing, pressing my nipples into the spandexed give of my yoga top. I waited for a direction to indicate that I wanted her to touch me for the entire class. She didn't offer that option.

She wasn't typically my type. Anyone who knew me knew I had a predilection for short men with enthusiastic dicks. He shaved his head. I nipped it and licked it with a slow languor when he wound magic knuckled fingers through every fold of my cunt.

He had deflowered me years after I'd lost my virginity. Years lost to uneventful fondling and generic penetration. He ripped away each of my reserves, one torturously delightful layer after another. Till now, every petal gone, I lay open to anything.

My little blonde attraction skated around the room, extolling us to stretch out our breath. I took six counts to drag in a breath that traversed my sensitized body like flood waters creeping into dry holes. It came to rest in my chest, beating against my nipples from the inside out. Sensually singeing them against the minute woven fibers cupping my breasts.

"Push up and roll over onto your hands and knees," she directed.

She appeared next to me. I saw her mauve painted toes: all straight with little bulbous ends. I swallowed, closing my eyes and imagining suckling each one into my mouth while her face changed in waves. From breath-held surrender to the languid moan of abandoned reserve. She would hold out as long as she could before she shuddered into me.

Her hand palmed my backbone as she lured the class to round their backs like cats, then drop their bellies. Breasts pressing, asses cocked high. We repeated that rocking motion six times.

Her hand flexed and gripped, kneading my backbone into a rhythmic undulation. It trailed closer to my ass each time I arched it into the air, finding the ridge right before my crack. Leaving a fingerprint of sensation.

Her next command—to walk or softly jump to the top of our mats and hang in a forward fold—sounded like it came from the upper-right corner of the rectangular studio. I rolled my head in her direction, expecting to see her reflected in the tall mirrors resting against the right hand wall.

But she was everywhere in the room, pacing and slinking around the lined-up mats. Bent double, blood and desire raced to my head. I swayed, trancelike. Heady. Euphoric.

My cunt clenched when her fingers started at my ankles and roamed up the backs of my legs, taking their sweet, fluttery time as she pushed me deeper into the fold, stretching my taut hamstrings with the barest pressure of her palm.

She exhaled the suggestion to "breathe" in a hot moist gust against the back of my knee. My breath released in a gush. When I drew in a long draught of lavender and cypress scented air, she finished her fingering climb up the back of my thighs, stopping, but pulling away with a linger.

Small brushfires traced the path she'd made up my legs. The room misted over. Diaphanous clouds of fog cloaked the rest of the class. I could see them move in slow motion, but they were blind in their own yogic trances.

I closed my eyes and sank into the thigh-strengthening discipline of Warrior Two. Torso turned sideways, right leg bent at a right angle to the floor, I sank into a lunge. She pressed her body into the back of mine, sinking to mimic my pose. Her cunt tilted up against my ass. I wanted her to grow a dick and fuck me.

My arms were outstretched, making airplane wings. She trickled her palms from my fingertips to my shoulders, leaving a forest of prickling hair and a moonscape of goosebumps. The journey took her back around my shoulder blades, across the damp of my armpits, and then her fingernails coasted across the soft underbelly of my arms to clasp my palms, weaving her fingers into mine.

My right thigh burned, but I complied when she asked me to bend it deeper. I sent breath into the fire to both soothe and stoke. We completed a Sun Salutation, landing in Warrior Two again, this time with our left legs bent and my body rotated to face her.

She moved my left arm a tiny fraction higher, using this minute adjustment to plaster herself against me, mirroring my pose. She goaded me to sink further into the strength of my left leg.

It burned and whined.

She grated up against me, her breasts arrowing into mine. Our puckered nipples connected like magnets. We breathed in tandem. Six long, slow counts on the inhale; then six, shuddering beats as we let the air escape.

She rocked forward and back in minute teasing motions. My chest festered with feeling.

Then she disappeared, taking our heated connection away with her next exhortation to the class. The coolness she left shivered through me.

"Windmill your hands to frame your left foot . . ." Her voice hypnotized me through a series of movements bringing me into Downward Dog, a resting pose for seasoned yogis. It was a restless pose for me today.

Body stretched into a human V, I pressed into my hands, lifting my hips in the air and inviting her attention. Shackles pinned my wrists and ankles to my mat. My black yoga pants, slick with my stimulation, disappeared. I paused naked. Open. Available.

I felt her behind me, taking me in. Her long, slow exhale released a fluid dance on the curly hair covering my cunt. I kept it long and untamed: wild.

Her breath reminded me of his. When he roamed that intimate opening, he combed my pubic curls and used them to pull my lips apart—wide. Or he brushed my bush with the barest pass of his palm. It milked me, making me brim.

But nothing he ever did felt like the living heat of her breath worming through me and prying me apart. I wanted to stay forever in this obeisance, untouched and aching for it.

She breathed in, six more long counts, sniffing me as if I was freshly baked bread.

He said I smelled like musky, flowered honey. He reveled in it, bringing his slickened fingers under my nose before slathering my tongue with my own heat.

I pressed back, deeper in the pose, furthering my vulnerable offering. I wanted her to worship me or ravage me—strap on something long and thick that would plunder farther than his cock could reach.

"Now drop your knees and settle back in Child's Pose," she directed.

The shackles disappeared, the room came back into focus, and my legs trembled. I lowered into another prayer, splaying my knees wide so my belly and breasts could sink to the mat. My arms reached over my head.

This is where yogis go when they want to catch their breath, rest, and recover. I sank into this refuge with gratitude, panting and yearning. I used it to mask the way my breathing rushed in and out of my lungs, burying the want my nipples couldn't hide. Yet, craving, I rubbed them along the texture of my mat.

She dropped her knees on my ass, pressing me deeper into the bend. Her hands roamed my upper back and shoulders, oozing and soothing. She skimmed my sides.

My pussy pulsed. I swallowed, imagining the saliva that puddled on my tongue was her gush. When she left me to administer her blessing on another bent soul, my body stayed supine, ripening.

He would learn a few things tonight—about ravaging.

We did our balance pose then. On good days, my balance sucked. My mind roamed, likely because my pervasive throb didn't allow me to find the right equation between want and need. And when I focused, my trying so hard made me wobble.

She called for Dancer, a lovely shape for the body to bend in to.

At her command, I strengthened my left leg, bent my right knee, and searched for the top of my foot with my right palm. I stood stork-like and steady.

"This may be your pose today, and if so, this will give your quad the stretch it needs. If you are ready to move to the next stage, raise your left arm and tilt forward."

I ventured into the cant, reaching forward with my left fingertips and pulling with my right palm, leveraging my right leg into a high curve. I soared. The pose split my pussy into a sacrament.

I stayed without trying. Solid. Deft. Alight. Her hands hovered to catch me if I fell.

On cue, I unraveled into Mountain pose, coming back to stillness with a greased grace and an economy of movement.

She urged us to find our Dancer on the right leg. This time I quaked and wobbled, my mind racing with pride and the pressure in my cunt.

Her hands steadied me, pressing with a surety into my left thigh, thumb twitching perilously close to the wet sog of my crotch. She arched me into an impossible curve. Holding me there until my mind let go of the effort.

My legs trembled when we settled back into our Mountain. Adrenalin rattled my bones. At her command, I dove into another Forward Fold. My head teeming from the blood rush, I swayed, fingers drawing an imaginary arc around my rooted feet. I brushed the mat with the same spiritual lightness I wanted to enlist to explore her.

We dropped down to our backs to stretch and twist before we sank into our final resting pose. My muscles throbbed into repose, surrendering.

I lay supine on a hard floor. Body and mind were floating in a state between sleep and perception.

She touched us all after oiling her sleek fingers and palms with some heady aromatherapy mixture and kneading our feet.

I waited for the sound of her. She set the glass bottle down with the slightest click against the wooden floor. Her knee would crack as she bent, and my skin would rise to her touch, begging it to stay.

I arched in anticipation, and a tiny orgasm shimmered through me. I suppressed the attendant moan.

On the back row, I released and drowsed in my enlightened state for long minutes before I had to deal with her touch—before I had to make myself lie still and stop myself from grabbing those oiled hands and pulling her on top of me. Before starting with a tongue-infused kiss.

Soundless, without warning, her touch found the arch of each foot. I stifled a moan and worked it into a sigh. How could one simple touch be so electric?

She kneaded the insides of my feet, traveling heel to toe, building pressure. She always ended with a feather-light brush of her fingers across the tender skin on the top of my feet.

I loved and hated that sensation, knowing she would move on then to entice another soul into lying still and allowing her to leave them defenseless and wanting. Like me.

Her fingers surprised me. I sucked in a gasp, and this time the moan found its way past my lips. It rushed out hot and damp.

She prodded up my inner calves. I tightened and clenched my muscles into a near charley horse and tilted my cunt into her knead. She kept coming, her fingers digging a line of fire as they gentled the knobbiness of my inner knees.

I swallowed, tilting my pussy. I wanted to palm my nipples. I grabbed hold of the sides of my mat.

Her fingers crawled up my thighs in a taunt. Rubbing, swirling, swaying, probing. Stealing away any resistance. They met at the V of my legs and danced there together in my wet, slick core. I spasmed, warmth drenching my mat.

She backed away.

I raised up on my elbows, head falling back, watching her through the same slitted eyes that started this journey.

She sniffed her fingers with her long six-count breath, then drove two of them down her throat until she gagged. She lapped her fingers with her tongue, sucking me out from under her short manicured nails.

He will definitely learn something tonight.

I will manipulate and maneuver him with frightening intensity. I will strum him with this delicious depravity. I will fondle him without boundaries.

Make his eyes grow wide with sensation.

Fuck his soul loose.

Then cover his languid, heaving form with my own and meld into one.

Namaste.

✑ SWELLING TIDES ✑

Dorothy Tinker

THE FIRST TIME Tælen saw the redhead, he mistook him for a mere boy.

He'd been exploring the Pecalini marketplace after replenishing his ship's supplies when the snap of frustrated Fayralese amongst the flurry of fluid Pecalini caught his attention.

"I don' want *peas*! I wan' *beans*!"

Turning toward the words, Tælen raised his eyebrows at the sight of the thin lad gesturing wildly at the merchant. The boy tugged haplessly at his dark-red braid when the merchant only shook his head and offered him an open sack of dried peas.

"It's just Juan, up to his usual tricks," Voz whistled from her perch on Tælen's shoulder.

"Seems like it," Tælen responded in the tongue of the animals.

Just as Tælen was about to turn away from the scene, the redhead threw his braid over his shoulder and leaned closer to Juan, his teeth gritted as he hissed something too softly for Tælen to hear. When the merchant paled, the redhead's lips spread into a fierce grin that caught like a hook in Tælen's gut and made him stumble.

Voz squawked in his ear, but Tælen ignored her as he turned back to watch the redhead lean back and smirk. "Now, about those beans," he proclaimed.

As Juan dipped his head several times and began speaking in fluent Fayralese, Voz clamped her beak onto Tælen's earlobe. *"Don't see why you're suddenly so interested,"* she whistled, even as Tælen tapped her beak. *"So he managed to turn the tides on Juan. That's not unusual."*

Tælen shook his head once Voz had released his ear. *"Perhaps not for seasoned pirates like us, but . . ."* He glanced once more at the redhead before turning away. *"He's fiercer than I would have expected."*

※

The first time Dayphin noticed the man with the bird, he confused his silence for arrogance.

He'd spent nearly two hours haggling with Pecalini merchants to resupply his ship. Normally his first mate, who was fluent in Pecalini, would have taken the task, but he, and nearly half their crew, had become ill from spoiled food supplies. Hence the need to resupply.

Damn rats.

Unwilling to return to his ship and half-ill crew in such a rotten mood, Dayphin ducked into a tavern that he knew, from the yells and raucous laughter spilling forth from it, catered to men like him who were making port for only a day or two. Settling himself at the bar, he waved over the barkeep and soon had a tankard of ale in one hand and a roving eye on the surrounding crowd.

The crowd consisted of the usual sort: Burly men who were obviously ship laborers. Men of a lither stature, like Dayphin, who probably spent much of their time up in their ship's riggings. Even a few lads who couldn't be older than eleven or twelve.

"Those were the days," Dayphin muttered and turned away from the reminder of simpler times. He couldn't rightly say he missed them much, not when he was the captain of his own pirate ship, but there were times when he could wish for things to be as easy as they used to be.

He was staring into the dark depths of his ale when a sudden screech cut across his brooding thoughts. "Somethin' I can help you with?" quickly accompanied the screech, and Dayphin turned to find the source.

He blinked when he spotted a large red and blue bird bobbing fussily on the shoulder of a tall, neatly dressed man. Surrounding them stood five well-muscled ship laborers, all of whom glared up at the man and bird, though only one of them apparently had to guts to poke the taller man in the chest.

"Wouldn' do that if I were you."

Dayphin felt his jaw drop. *That was the bird?* He'd never heard of an animal that could speak like a human. The words had been accompanied by a whistle, and the tall man hadn't even twitched.

"Shut up, bird!" snapped the bravest of the laborers. "I'm talkin' to your human."

The bird bristled, but the neatly dressed man raised a hand and ran a single finger down the bird's breast feathers. The bird quickly settled, and the man tipped his head toward the laborer, obviously inviting him to speak.

This time the laborer bristled, and Dayphin noted with amusement that he did it almost as well as the bird had. "Canna you a' leas' say somet'in'?"

The tall man raised an eyebrow, and the bird softly whistled, "You wan' verbal acknowledgment from a human, you'll have to look elsewhere."

Dayphin winced and glanced away as the laborer snarled and lunged for the taller man. Refusing to respond to the laborer's demands was one thing, but allowing his bird to taunt the sturdier man was simply reckless.

And Dayphin wasn't in the mood to watch a pair of idiots fight.

Could have just returned to my ship if I wanted to do that.

A sudden bark of laughter startled Dayphin out of his thoughts. Lifting his gaze, he watched the barkeep shake his head. "Let 'im go, Taelen," he ordered, though the laughter in his voice belied the sternness of his words. "You canna expec' ever'one to recognize your Voz."

Frowning, Dayphin turned back toward the commotion. He blinked when he realized that the tall, neatly dressed man had full command of the situation. The attacking laborer was sprawled across a table, one arm twisted up behind his back. The neatly dressed man held him down with one hand, but his attention was on the men surrounding him, warning them off with narrowed eyes.

That his free hand was lifted to restrain the bird bobbing silently on his shoulder rather than the four other men impressed Dayphin more than the strength implied by his easy grip on his attacker.

"¡Discúlpate!" the bird snapped after a long moment of silence. Dayphin started as he realized that the bird was now speaking Pecalini. "¡O acepta una batalla de barcos!"

Laughter sounded behind Dayphin even as the tall man flicked a finger against the bird's breast. The bird ruffled its feathers but didn't glance away from the pinned man.

"The lot o' ye should apologize," the barkeep added, humor still tinging his words. "Don' know 'ow, but ye managed to rile Voz enough that she's threatenin' a battle o' ships, an' I don' think any o' ye wanna be explainin' to tus capitanes why they're bein' challenged by the Silent Raider."

The four laborers shifted and traded glances and even the pinned man tensed upon hearing the barkeep's words. Dayphin himself raised his eyebrows. He had heard of the Silent Raider. He didn't know who the captain was, but he knew it was a pirate ship similar to his own Wind Runner.

"'M sorry, sir," muttered one of the laborers, dropping his head into a short bow. "We didn' mean to offend with our questions, an' we shouldn've attacked ye." He motioned to his fellows, who murmured their own apologies and backed off.

The tall man watched the group silently for a long moment before nodding and releasing his attacker. The bird squawked something more in Pecalini, but the man only shook his head and motioned for the laborers to leave.

Once they were gone, he turned to the bar and nodded to the barkeep. The bird ruffled its feathers, glanced at the tall man with a look that Dayphin could only describe as a glare, and then squawked, "Apologies, Javier. Didn't mean to make trouble in your establishment."

"Nonsense," the barkeep answered. "Personas don' 'ave the righ' to deal in Pecali if they don' know better than to insult una lora."

Dayphin frowned at the unfamiliar word as the bird lifted its beak and rustled its feathers. The tall man shook his head, a small smile playing on his lips, before he poked the bird in the breast feathers once more. "Apologies, anyway," the bird whistled, and then they disappeared through the tavern door.

Dayphin stared at the door for long moments after the man with the bird left. The man's silent strength had been impressive, but Dayphin still thought it was arrogant of him to remain silent at all times, even when speaking would have saved him a fight.

Heat suddenly warmed Dayphin's face, and he bit his lip. *Of course, when he can subdue a man that easily. . . .*

A warm chuckle from behind Dayphin dragged his attention away from the door and his thoughts, and he turned to find the barkeep—Javier—smiling at him.

"I take it ye've ne'er met Capitán Tælen afore, chiquito."

Dayphin narrowed his eyes, unimpressed with the diminutive address—one of the few phrases he knew in Pecalini. "I'll have you know that I'm a pirate captain in my own right." Then the man's other words registered, and he faltered. "Wait. He was . . . ."

Glancing over his shoulder at the door, Dayphin slid his red braid over his other shoulder and tugged at it. "He's a pirate captain?"

"Sí, despite 'is disability."

Dayphin's head snapped around so quickly he winced and rubbed at his neck. "Disability? What disability?"

Javier raised an eyebrow. "Surely you noticed he couldn't speak."

Dayphin opened his mouth and then hesitated. "Couldn't?" he finally whispered.

The barkeep nodded. "Sí. Tælen was born mute. Es only 'is Magia Animal an' 'is lora, Voz, that let 'im speak 'is mente."

Dayphin glanced back at the door. "You mentioned loras earlier. Is that the bird?"

Javier chuckled. "You really don' know much abou' Pecali, do you?" Dayphin glared at the barkeep, who only shrugged in response. "Loros are inteligentes an' can be found throughout the rainforest, but it's a rare loro that befriends un humano. To insult one is to invite the wrath o' no' only its entire flock, bu' that of any criaturas mágicas it 'as befriended."

Shaking his head, he added, "That those hombres were tantos enough to insult una lora that considers herself una pirata as well."

Raising his tankard to his lips, Dayphin considered the barkeep's words. If this Captain Tælen really couldn't speak and was dependent solely on the friendship of a bird to communicate with other humans. . . .

The memory of the way the silent man had held up a hand to restrain the lora instead of the surrounding laborers rose in Dayphin's mind, and he shivered. *Such confidence. Such strength.*

Dayphin tried to drown the thoughts in his ale, but the silent captain refused to leave his thoughts, even after he returned to his ship and half-ill crew.

—◊◊◊—

The first time Tælen spoke with the redhead, the younger man saved his life.

It wasn't the Silent Raider's finest moment when two Fayralese warships, the Giorsal and the Buadhachan, caught Tælen and his crew unawares on a foggy day. Before Tælen could even order his men to man the battle fires, they were boarded by overwhelming numbers. Voz managed two sets of orders before five men surrounded Tælen and brought him to his knees.

Hours later, the Giorsal pulled away from the Raider laden with most of her cargo, leaving the Buadhachan to deal with punishing Tælen and his men. Most of the Raider's crew had been secured below deck, but the Buadhachan's captain, an elven warrior by the name of Dubhloach, insisted on dealing with Tælen above deck.

Dubhloach lifted the cage they'd stuffed Voz into and peered in at her coldly. "It amazes me, Captain," he spoke clearly, "that a man as rough as yourself could present a loro anything worthy enough to gain its friendship."

Voz squawked and flapped her wings as violently as she could in the cramped space and cursed at the Fayralese elf in Pecalini. The elf merely raised an eyebrow and waved a hand toward the cage. Tælen stiffened as he felt a wave of Animal Magic engulf the cage, silencing Voz as effectively as separating her from Tælen silenced him.

"Much better," Dubhloach said, handing the cage off to a subordinate. "It is the height of rudeness to speak in a tongue those around you cannot understand." He smirked down at Tælen, who knelt at his feet with his arms chained behind his back. "Then again, perhaps it is ruder still to steal the voice of one's enemy. But then," he added, slipping a dagger from his belt, "who would care when that enemy is a pirate?"

Tælen held the elf's gaze as he pressed his blade to Tælen's throat. Tælen might have lost command of his ship, crew, and voice, but he refused to let the Fayralese captain steal his control of his own body and emotions. If Tælen were to die here and now, it would not be in cowering fear.

He barely twitched when pain bloomed beneath the elf's cold blade, only his shoulders tightening against the threat of death. Still, Dubhloach's smirk turned crueler yet, and he began to drag the blade across Tælen's throat, only to stumble back when a sudden explosion burst against their ears and rocked the Silent Raider beneath his boots. Tælen didn't bother looking to see what had exploded. For all he knew, the Buadhachan had fired battle fires upon his ship. Instead, he sprung at Dubhloach, shoving his shoulder into the elf's gut and knocking him to the ground. A cry sounded behind him and he lurched to one side, turning to watch one of the elf's subordinates stumble past him as he evaded their attack.

"Captain!" another Fayralese soldier shouted before a second explosion drowned out whatever he might have said.

Chaos erupted then as Tælen ducked and dodged attacks, using his feet and shoulders to retaliate when he could. More soldiers appeared from below deck, though from the muffled shouts that followed them, those they'd left behind quickly learned why so many of them had been set to guard Tælen's crew. More explosions shook the ship, but it didn't take Tælen long to realize that it wasn't his ship taking damage.

Screams from the direction of the Buadhachan only confirmed that.

"She's going down!" someone shouted minutes later. For a long, dangerous moment, the Silent Raider tilted toward the sinking ship as the ropes tied between the two ships threatened to take the Raider down with the Buadhachan, but the sharp *snap* of breaking lines and *crack* of breaking wood was quickly followed by a sharp pitch in the opposite direction. Cries sounded from those who hadn't expected the sudden movement, quickly followed by yells of victory as Tælen's crew took the advantage.

Minutes later, Tælen stood above Dubhloach, a sword in one hand and Voz perched on the opposite shoulder. Around him, his men were binding the surviving Fayralese.

"Well, Captain," Voz squawked, "have anything to say now?"

The elf sneered. "You will regret this, pirate." He turned to look across the Raider's deck and raised his voice so everyone could hear. "I have already sent a message by animal to the Giorsal. She will return and—"

"Wouldn' be so certain o' that, Dubhloach."

Tælen turned, startled, to find the thin redhead he'd once mistaken for a boy sauntering across the Raider's deck. Behind him, just visible through the fog, another ship floated peacefully beside the Raider.

"Afternoon, Captain Tælen," the redhead greeted with a grin. "Thought you migh' wan' some help."

Tælen raised an eyebrow. "You sank the Buadhachan?" Voz squawked, ruffling her feathers. To Tælen, she whistled, *"You don't have to feel* that *much appreciation toward him."*

He ignored her as the redhead bobbed his head. "Aye, my crew and I." Offering his hand to Tælen, he added, "Captain Dayphin of the Wind Runner."

Tælen's other eyebrow joined the first as he took Dayphin's hand. *Captain? At such a young age?*

"Dayphin Strongweather?" Dubhloach spat. "You were under the control of the Onora when I last saw you!"

The redhead blinked golden brown eyes and turned to stare at the elf. "Aye," he answered after a long moment, "bu' you seem to forget tha' the Fayralese aren' well-liked among us pirates. Captain Orphus o' the Silver Girl sank the Onora afore her captain could even consider our punishment, an' he agreed to an alliance with me to hunt you down.

"Course," he added with an apologetic glance at Tælen, "he demanded first run at the loot, which is why he wen' after the Giorsal. I'm afraid you won' be gettin' all your cargo back, Captain Tælen."

Tælen shook his head, though he had to nudge Voz to speak up in answer. "Wasn't expecting to have the life and freedom of my crew an hour ago. Part of our cargo is small enough payment for those."

Dayphin nodded and turned back to Dubhloach. Tælen didn't need Voz's beak on his ear to know that the sudden burning in his chest and the desire to turn the redhead's gaze back to him were both stupid. Unfortunately, they all occurred anyway.

"Now," Dayphin said, "what were you thinkin' o' doin' with the fine elf captain, if you don' mind me askin'?"

Tælen glanced down at Dubhloach and shook his head. "Would throw him overboard if he didn't have access to Animal Magic." Voz accompanied the words with a glare.

Dayphin nodded. "Could be problematic, that." He sucked his bottom lip in between his teeth, and Tælen swallowed and glanced away. "Runnin' him through would jus' be messy, 'specially since the battle's already over."

Tælen nodded, his eyes already shifting back to the redhead. To his surprise, the other man's golden brown eyes met him straight on before glancing away. Tælen blinked as red spread quickly across the redhead's nose and cheeks, warming Tælen's belly in a way he hadn't expected.

"Maybe," Dayphin muttered thickly and then cleared his throat. "Maybe we can jus' slit his throat as we drop him overboard." He lifted his gaze, though not high enough to meet Tælen's eyes. "Seems only righ' to repay the favor o' what he tried to do to you."

Tælen frowned, wondering how the redhead knew that Dubhloach had tried to slit his throat. Voz refused to ask, but she apparently didn't need to as Dayphin met his gaze and touched his own throat. "You've got . . ." he began and then reached his hand up to Tælen's throat.

Tælen inhaled sharply when the redhead's fingers brushed against his skin, and a shiver swept down his spine. Immediately Dayphin pulled back, an apology on his lips and in his eyes. Tælen swallowed and shook his head to deny the pain Dayphin apparently believed he was in, though he had to clench his fists behind his back to keep from touching his throat in turn.

"The idea has merit," Voz squawked, hoping to distract Tælen. The sideways glance she gave him in the next moment told the silent captain that she knew it hadn't worked.

"Still don't see why he excites you so."

Of course you don't, Tælen responded silently. *I'm only figuring that out myself.*

—⁓—

The first time Dayphin kissed Tælen, the world exploded with color.

No one liked to miss Mid-Season Day celebrations, and the crew of the Wind Runner was no exception. The festivals took place four times a year, and Dayphin tried to visit a different port in each season—partly to avoid capture, partly to enjoy the different ways countries celebrated the holy days.

This winter, Dayphin and his crew had chosen to visit Celania. The island country was small, but with the size of their shipping and fishing economy, it was easy for pirate ships to blend in among the ports.

They'd docked two days before Mid-Winter Day to give Dayphin and his men time to sell their cargo, so it was with a light heart and mind that Dayphin woke on Mid-Winter morning. Leaving his men behind at the inn, the redhead wandered farther into the city, excited to enjoy the festivities.

He spent hours watching sword fights, boxing matches—an unexpected treat since Dayphin had thought the sport restricted to the mainland—fire eaters, street acrobats, and even a display of magical birds that enthralled Dayphin more than he would have thought possible.

He was stumbling away from admiring the red and blue blaze of a phoenix's flames when another flash of red and blue caught his eye. Blinking in confusion, Dayphin snapped his head around to figure out what he had just seen, but whatever it was had been lost in the crowd.

Several hours later, he was still pondering the flash of blue and red as he wandered back toward the docks. The sun would be setting soon, and the seas would come alive as the celebration moved out of the city and onto the docks and ships. For some reason, though, Dayphin wasn't as excited as he had been. The last few hours had felt oddly empty, but Dayphin couldn't place why.

He was beginning to wonder if he should simply return to the inn—or perhaps even the Wind Runner—when hands suddenly caught his shoulders and his vision was filled with red and blue.

"Watch your step!" squawked a familiar voice, and Dayphin gasped as he realized that Captain Tælen stood right in front of him, the red and blue Voz bobbing quickly on his shoulder.

"Tælen! Gods, sorry, I—" Dayphin shook his head and took a step back, though he had to swallow as the silent man's hands slid slowly off his shoulders. They had run into each other several times since the incident with the Buadhachan, and each encountered seemed to involve more touching and more unusual sensations than the last. "Sorry, I've been a bit distracted."

Tælen's gray eyes, which looked nearly black in the waning sunlight, grew concerned. "Something wrong?" Voz whistled. She'd stopped bobbing, and the eye she trained on him looked nearly as concerned as Tælen's. The sight had Dayphin smiling and shaking his head before he could even consider it.

"Nay, nothin's wrong. I jus' haven' been as comfortable as I'd like." Deciding to take a risk, he met Tælen's eyes, raised his chin, and murmured, "Been missin' somethin'."

Tælen's eyes darkened, and Voz chirruped wordlessly. Then, much to Dayphin's surprise, Voz twisted her neck and buried her beak in the feathers at her back. Before he could ask if something was wrong with her, Tælen stepped closer and slid a hand up over Dayphin's jaw, stealing his words and his breath.

The silent captain held him like that for several heartbeats, simply staring into Dayphin's eyes. Dayphin was nearly chewing on his lower lip by the time he smiled and brushed his lips against Dayphin's.

Dayphin groaned as fire shot down his spine and pooled in his belly. His lips tingled, his fingers caught in the linen of Tælen's tunic, and he leaned against the other man in a silent request for more.

Tælen's chest shook beneath Dayphin's fingers—his silent laughter—before the older pirate parted his lips and soothed a line of wetness over Dayphin's bottom lip.

Dayphin cursed. He couldn't help it. Throwing an arm over the shoulder not holding Voz, he pressed himself closer to Tælen and opened himself to the older man as much as he could.

Tælen did not disappoint.

Warmth and strength plunged into Dayphin's mouth, and he groaned again as he pressed back, refusing to simply take it. Teeth cut into lips, tongues pressed against cheeks, and all the while, heat pooled between them in an all-too-unmistakable way.

Dayphin was beginning to think that they both were wearing too much clothing when a sudden explosion rocked through him and red burst across his eyelids.

Jerking his head back, Dayphin threw open his eyes and stared around in search of the explosion. A second later, he barked out a laugh as another explosion of color lit the sky, this time in a joyous blue that made the sky look briefly like the phoenix he had seen earlier in the day.

Or Voz.

"Don' suppose you've been offerin' the Fire Masters inspiration for their displays," he muttered, poking the lora in the breast feathers. She lifted her head, took one look at the sky, which was already being lit with skyfires of other colors, and squawked, "No yo." In the next moment, she buried her beak in her back feathers once more.

Dayphin raised his eyebrows and glanced at Tælen. He had learned that Voz only spoke in Pecalini when she was speaking her own words, and her current curtness surprised him.

One look at Tælen's face, however, stole away any concerns he might have had. His eyes, heavy and intense, met Dayphin's directly, and the redhead pressed forward, his lips forming an offer to move to his ship before his thoughts could fully assess it.

Perhaps, he thought as he led Tælen toward the Wind Runner's dock, *the skyfires won't be the only explosions tonight.*

SIBLING RIVALRY

Elizabeth Ann Domino

HIS LIPS WERE the most amazing shade of crimson, not true crimson, but that shade of raspberry that comes right before crimson, reminding me of a grapefruit. And when he moistened . . . let's just say there weren't enough paper towels to take care of that mess. And his eyes . . . there is no way to do them justice verbally. It requires guttural slurping noises and flaying of my hands, moaning, eyes rolled back. Deep, deep green. A chartreuse, with just a hint of gold. Flecks similar to a feline—seductive and intriguing all at once.

Come-fuck-me eyes had been eyeing me all night long. Sitting clad in cling-wrap ebony leather pants and a cerulean blue button down, he seemed indecisive about making the first move. I kept glancing up from my stool, hoping my perfectly tweezed eyebrows exhibited the intentions I had—that I wanted him to take me home and make my eyes roll back in my head. That I wanted the breeder bitch next door who complained about the loud bass of Paul Oakenfold, my choice of fluorescent attire and penchant for silver eyeliner, to hear every moan, scream, and sigh. The pumping dance beat and technology-enhanced echoing vocals of Cher filled the club, the heat from the sweating gyrating bodies on the dance floor creating a sweaty fog that was slowly creeping into our end of the bar. I could feel the heat of his eyes on the back of my neck, and I realized he had gotten up from the bar stool and was now headed my way.

I gulped my martini as fast as I could and stood up so quickly he stopped for a second before heading the five more feet to close the gap. He did not have to speak; he grabbed my hand and I followed him to the exit, praying to God this wasn't some guy's idea of a joke and that tomorrow on the 7 o'clock news my mother wouldn't hear about the mangled and beaten body of a thin white boy found dumped in an alley. Poor little Christopher Beret. "What happened to that fine youth?" my mother would moan and cry as my father damned me to hell. No I couldn't become some scraped-up fag sent to the morgue of Parker hospital, especially since my sister was introducing the family to her newest victim, I mean mate. God forbid I miss that. I would never hear the end. Never mind I might have exhibited poor judgment and ended up with a Jeffrey Dahmer on my hands. No, I couldn't disappoint my mother and big sis.

I'll tell you what happened to that fine youth: I spent the night with the best piece of ass I have ever had in my thirty-one years on this planet. God knows we queens are prone to exaggeration, but this was the most amazing sex. The things this man could do with his tongue . . . his hands took me to the edge of something I cannot describe, at least, not without getting thrown in jail or at the very least paid $2.99 a minute. Maybe not a bad idea. He brought wave after wave of pleasure, wave after wave of . . . of something I can't name because I don't know if there is a word—a word for something that primal, that raw. Maybe there is, but only in Hustler.

Needless to say, Chartreuse, as I had begun to call him (because we never got around to the formality of names), rocked my world. Come morning I did not want to give him up, but everyone knows it's better to kick 'em out before the Cinderella fantasy tarnishes. Besides, I had a death-by-family brunch I had to subject myself to. The last thing I needed was a stranger left in my apartment and me with no stereo or TV to come home to. Even good sex can't cure a pissed off and vengeful gay man whose shit has been stolen. No, he had to leave, and now.

We said our goodbyes—over and over and over. I finally managed to catch a taxi toward uptown, leaving him standing, waiting for the next one.

Twenty-five minutes later, due to a busted water main and a cabbie who couldn't speak English (or as he put it, Village English), I arrived at the café where I could see my sister and mother deep in conversation with a tall man. I made my way to the table just as he glanced up. He stared at me with the most beautiful eyes I had ever seen: a deep green. Deep chartreuse, one might say.

〜◎ LOVE LETTERS FROM THE HEART ◎〜
Bernard Young

*"Love and magic have a great deal in common. They enrich
the soul, delight the heart, and they both take practice."*
—*Nora Roberts*

OSCAR, MY TEMPORARY "big brother," had spent the night with me before my departure to London and Europe. It had been a sad parting since we disliked the thought of not seeing each other for the next few weeks. We did our best to keep ourselves in good spirits when we said our goodbyes the following morning. As much as Oscar did not welcome the idea of spending our holidays separately and me going with my valet, he donned a brave face and wished me an enjoyable vacation. He reminded me that I would be on his mind throughout our time apart. As much as I wanted to spend the holidays with Oscar, I had responsibilities to fulfill: spending a little time in London with Uncle James and the rest of the two and half weeks with Andy, visiting our professor friends, Ludwig and Oberon, i n Baden Württemberg, Germany. I had also promised Andy to visit his parents in Vaduz on Christmas and Boxing Day.

The evening after my saviors rescued me from the horrific clutches of the robbers, we had spent the night sleeping together on the same bed. None of my three "bears" wanted me alone. I was petrified during the frightening assault and was glad my protectors were next to me on either side as if they were guarding a precious jewel. Andy had washed and cleaned me in a hot bath before wrapping his cozy red-and-black-checkered flannel bathrobe around my shivering body. He tucked me between Ludwig, Oberon, and himself in the king-size bed. Sandwiched between my three sexy bears, their warmth radiating from their naked bodies, I felt safe. Wrapped in Andy's hairy chest, a peaceful loving sensation fell across my tired eyes before sensual and sexual thoughts began drifting through my mind. The evening's excitements were too terrifying and I was lucky to be saved by these three hunky angels now keeping watch, holding and caring for my safety. Their masculinity aroused as I held tightly onto my lover while his intoxicating scent drifted up my nostrils. Before long, my valet had lowered his face to mine, gently kissing my longing lips and desiring mouth. Surrendering to his loving touch, I was grateful for his protection.

Oberon lay against my back, his muscular hands wrapped around my slender waist, and his palms began inching toward my throbbing erection. With his blonde pubic hair gliding against my backside, I couldn't resist tilting my lower back toward my rescuer's groin, his erection sliding against my opening. Feeling his breath on the back of my neck, he stuck his tongue out and lapped at my ear lobes. The erotic sensations were too tantalizing for the three of us. Turning on my back, I offered access to Oberon's wet lips, nibbling on my ears. Moving slowly down my left nipple, the blonde angel munched, licked, and ate at my tiny nob until it resembled a little ripe cherry on top of a delicious cake.

Andy, imitating the blonde's actions on my other side, caused me to moan in rapturous ecstasies in the quiet night. Ludwig, having lowered himself between my legs, was busy licking, eating, and nibbling at my globes before plunging his mouth on my straining erection. Delighted to repay my saviors, I gave myself willingly to their loving caresses. That night, the bears and I took turns making love with each other, happily surrendering to each other's tantalizing touches, not wanting these ecstatic sensations to end. We copulated many times over until the wee hours before succumbing to sleep in each other's embrace. I was indeed the luckiest boy at Das Jagdhaus that winter's evening.

We did not leave the comfort of the bed until late afternoon. The beauty of our endless lovemaking was too invigorating to get out of bed to into the cold of Tübingen city for nourishment. But our tummies needed feeding, so we reluctantly left the comfort of the King and showered together under a blanket of warm tinkling water in our host's spacious bathroom. The closeness of our nakedness was too irresistible for us not to make love again. The entanglements of our body parts were too titillating to forgo another intimate session, and we continued where we left off on the king.

It seems I could never repay my saviors enough. Longing to please every part of their enticing bodies, I went to town sucking and licking their engorged lollipops, which were pointing at my face. Each mouthful was as yummy as the next. We took turns wrapping our lips and mouths on each other's length, savoring every drop of our oozing liquid while warm aqua rained down our dripping heads. None of us wanted these intoxicating simulations to end as we rotated in front of each other, savoring the human bratwurst delicacies offered us. Leaning against the shower wall, I gave myself to my angels, tilting my longing sex toward their engorged organs as they mounted their faun with passionate devotions. Before long, they were sowing their juicy seeds within my sweet offering. I wanted them, I needed them, and I loved them. I was eager to reward my heroes with love and gratitude for their unwavering grace.

By the time we got into Oberon's candy-apple-red 1966 Mercedes Benz W110, we were famished. Andy and I had situated ourselves warmly at the back of the vehicle as we drove to Weinstube Forelle, a historical German restaurant in old Tübingen city for a scrumptious Gulaschsuppe (Goulash soup) and Knackwurst with krauf meal, followed by a delicious Apfelstrudel (apple strudel) dessert.

Over brunch Andy inquired, "When does ChocolART start?"

Ludwig replied wickedly, "It starts tomorrow. There will be plenty to do and lots of sweet delicacies to eat! It's an all-you-can-eat buffet." He was licking his lips, already planning our erotic liaisons for when we returned to the cabin.

Oberon chimed in, adding flavor to his lover's naughty remarks, "By the end of the festival, you guys will be so full and will not want to get out of bed."

"You two have everything planned, haven't you?" Andy joked.

Ludwig laughingly continued, "Tomorrow we'll go to town for brunch and do some sightseeing before proceeding to the ChocolART Festival. How does that sound?"

"Fabulous!" I chirped in, "That sounds absolutely delicious. Everything is so sex-citing. What are we doing after brunch?"

Both hosts and Andy laughed at my childish exuberance before Oberon spoke. "Well, young man, you'll have to wait and see. Whatever we are doing will be very sex-citing," he said and continued laughing.

By now their contagious laughter had me in stitches, and I was amused at my own childish naiveté.

Our scrumptious food arrived, and I gobbled everything before me. Ravished from our excessive lovemaking, I was game to paint Tübingen red.

After the delicious meal, Ludwig suggested we visit the Eberhard Karls University where he and Oberon taught. The campus consisted of several outlying buildings/ Some were located in the old town, while other faculties were on campus. As the two professors showed us the institution, I reached into my shoulder bag to find my camera for some photo-ops. Instead I found an envelope tucked between my camera and a book. Since I didn't want to open the letter in front of my friends, I waited, suspecting the letter to be from Oscar. At Ludwig's office, while they were busy chatting, I excused myself to the rest facility. Inside a locked stall, I peeled open the envelope and a sparkling Christmas card emerged. It read:

Young, my dearest boy,

I miss you terribly. Life isn't the same without you. By the time you open this card, you will be in Germany and I in Scotland. I wish I could spend Christmas and New Year with you, Andy, and your friends. It would be fun! Unfortunately, my parents required my presence during the holiday season, leaving me little choice but home in Edinburgh with family. I look forward to seeing you at Daltonbury Hall in a couple of weeks, holding, caressing, and making love to you again. Your sexy groans never fail to excite my horny self, and I'm a selfish lover. I hope you are thinking of me daily. Be safe, and have a wonderful Christmas and a Happy New Year!

Love and kisses to my teddy bear!

Yours Truly,

Oscar

How could I not fall in love with my angelic big brother when he wrote so romantically? We were playing an emotionally dangerous game, and I felt terribly guilty not telling Andy the truth about my affair with this deliriously loving beau.

———⁓∾⁓———

Vaduz, Germany

It was a sunny Christmas Day in Vaduz. After a hearty, home-cooked break-fast by Frauline Maria, the twins, Andy, and I decided to go cross-country skiing. Arriving on a horse-drawn sleigh in the foothills of Vaduz Castle, we decided to ski back to the Finckenstein's cottage, which was approximately three miles south of the castle. Since Ari and Aria were avid skiers, they went ahead, opening a chance for me to talk with Andy of the issues that were gripping me hostage.

I asked, "Are you enjoying home?"

Sidestepping my question, my valet answered, "It's great to take time away to enjoy our holidays together. I'm glad my family likes you, although I can't tell my parents the truth about us. On the surface they are very polite to you, but I don't know what they are thinking."

"Your parents seem nice," I said. "I know your brother and sister are fine with us being a couple."

Andy continued with a sigh. "There are times I want to tell my parents I'm gay, but I don't think they will take kindly to my honesty. I hate not being open about our relationship. I love you dearly and would certainly like them to love and accept you as I do."

"I'm sure the correct moment will reveal itself for you to come clean. After all, we are here another day before returning to Daltonbury Hall. It seems pointless to stir up problematic resentment during our visit," I replied comfortingly.

"But Father pesters me about girlfriends whenever I'm home. I wish I could find the right moment to confide the truth about my sexuality, but it is none of my parents' business."

As we skied, I was figuring out how best to break my secret to Andy, so I responded calmly, "I'm sure it will be a shocker if you confess. Maybe it's best for them to find out for themselves; then they can decide how best to cope with the situation. You know I love you dearly and will never intentionally hurt you in any way."

Andy stopped skiing, looked at me, and said, "Uh-oh! What confessions do you have to make this time? I can tell you are up to something when you start professing your love for me and not wanting to hurt me. Well, boy, what dark secrets are you hiding? You better own up, mister!"

"I've been meaning to tell you the truth, but the right moment never seemed to manifest. My guilt has been festering like a sore, and I can't hide it anymore. Will you promise not to be angry with me?" I finally spoke.

Andy said in a loving voice, "You know I am not the angry type, and I don't harbor resentment for long. I am glad you are plucking up the courage to confess whatever you are hiding. Go on—spit it out, boy! I'm all ears. I'm listening."

With that encouragement, I told my lover the truth about my affair with Oscar. I told Andy repeatedly that I loved him very, very much and that nobody could ever replace him. He listened attentively as we slowly progressed along the ski trail, him saying nothing. I kept apologizing for not being truthful, asking his forgiveness. After going some distance, my valet stopped and spoke. "I'm not mad at you for loving Oscar; I've always had my suspicions regarding the two of you. It is noble to love but definitely not honorable to lie. I am terribly angry with you for lying, but not for loving Oscar. Love is a noble act, but lying—lying is a dreadful sin!"

I kept quiet, lost for words while figuring how best to respond. Finally I plucked up my courage and said, "My dilemma is that I love both of you equally.

I don't know what to do! I don't want to give up either of you; I want you both in my life."

Andy broke up with roaring laughter and replied, "That's an easy solution: We can have a triplet relationship. I don't blame you for loving Oscar; he is a charming guy, and since he loves you and I do too, the three of us together we can have a love fest. Do you think him agreeable to that? I am!"

I was caught speechless, not knowing how to respond to this unorthodox suggestion. I certainly did not anticipate such an unusual response. This was an unexpected surprise and certainly a solution to consider seriously; a solution I had never thought of before.

Before I could find the appropriate words to respond, Andy continued lovingly, "I am definitely open to loving Oscar and you, if we all agree. That way we can be happy together without having to keep secrets from each other.

"But you, young man, I am terribly disappointed in your constant dishonesty. This is a serious issue you must overcome. I have always told you that the truth will set you free. You can always confide in me. Let there be no secrets between us anymore. You understand?"

Feeling irresponsibly guilty, I nodded, informing my lover that I would seriously consider his triplet relationship suggestion and would have an answer for him before our vacation was over. I also solemnly promised him to not keep secrets from him in the future.

It was a tradition in Andy's German Jewish family to celebrate Yuletide with an elaborate family dinner. Frauline Maria and her daughter had been busy preparing a delicious meal for her family that evening. Herr Finckenstein, the patriarch, was happy to have his children home and asked about their dating lives over dinner. When it came to Andy's turn, my valet diverted the topic to other newsworthy events of the day instead of providing his father answers.

Ari tactfully came to his brother's rescue, saying, "Dad, if Andy isn't ready to divulge any information, don't pester him about whom he is dating. I'm sure he will inform you when he is ready."

Herr Finckenstein, turning to Andy, said impatiently, "Son, you can tell this old man."

I could detect annoyance in my valet's voice when he replied sarcastically, "It's none of your business, Dad, whom I am dating. I do not want to discuss this topic anymore." He then turned a deaf ear to his father's further questioning.

The room fell awkwardly silent for a several seconds before Aria changed the subject to break the eerie silence. "Dessert is ready. Shall we sit by the fire and have some liquor?"

The family's high spirits returned after we retreated to the living room. Andy, tipsy from drinking the wine and liquor, started dancing with his mother and sister to the radio's dance tunes. When a piece of romantic music came on the air, my lover pulled me off the sofa and we began slow dancing cheek to cheek, while his father desperately averted his gaze with much chagrin. Although the patriarch did not stop our dancing, I could detect extreme discomfort toward his son's act of defiance.

As the evening drew to a close, the siblings politely bid their parents Gute Nacht and retired to their respective chambers. Thinking Andy had securely locked our bedroom door, I fell into any intimate embrace with my lover on one of the single beds, snuggling close to his warm, muscular chest. That night I gave myself unselfishly to my lover as we consummated our love many times over, until exhaustion overshadowed our youthful bodies in a holy night of restful slumber.

Neither Andy nor I heard the knocking on our bedroom door until a loud crash shook us from our sleep. Frauline Maria stood, shocked and staring at our naked bodies intertwined on her son's bed. The breakfast trays she brought lay shattered, and the contents had splattered all over the carpet. For a brief moment I thought I was dreaming, but reality soon set in. I realized my lover had not locked the bedroom door. Had it been his intoxication, or had he purposely wanted his parents to discover us in bed? It was an answer I would never know. His mother had knocked, and after hearing no answer, pushed open the door intending to wake us gently for our respective breakfasts in our individual beds. Shocked by the sight of two naked interlocking boys on the same bed, she dropped the trays and woke the entire household in the process. Her husband and twins rushed to her aid, only to witness a still-naked Andy and me cuddled together. Yuletide hell had broken open its doors at Herr Egon Finckenstein's home. He now bore concrete evidence of his son's love interest, witnessing firsthand a shocked and scared boy of fourteen wrapped in his son's arms, face buried in his lover's chest.

"What are the two of you doing?" Egon demanded angrily.

Andy, awakened rudely by the commotion, rubbed his tired eyes and uttered, "What do you think we are doing?" As soon as my lover came to his senses, he grabbed the blanket, covering our nakedness from his parents' view.

The fuming patriarch spoke spitefully in a thunderous roar, "Get dressed immediately, and get the hell out of my house! *Now!*" He didn't give his son a chance to speak. Andy's mother pleaded with her husband not to make such any irrational decision, but the angry man refused to listen to his wife. Instead, he stomped into his den, locked the door, and stayed there until we left the house. The twins stood speechless, staring blankly at us. Finally Aria went over to console her mother while Ari cleaned the splattered mess.

Flashes of my clash with my father over my affair with KiWi returned with a vengeance. I knew the agony my lover was experiencing and did my best to console him with love and understanding. I quickly packed our belongings, ready to depart the Finckenstein home for good.

Dressed, Andy turned to me and said, "Let's get out of here now."

Without further ado, I did as was told. The twins tried to persuade us to stay, but their brother refused, muttering that he would not set foot in his father's house unless the old man apologized. If he couldn't accept his homosexuality, then they would never see each other again. As we loaded our luggage into our rental Volkswagen Beetle, Maria ran to embrace her son, pleading with him not to leave. Facing her tear-filled eyes, Andy said, "Mum, I love you very much and will miss you terribly, but I cannot stay after what happened. Dad obviously doesn't want us here. I will write you as soon as I return to school. I'll be in touch." After kissing his distraught mother on her cheeks and forehead, he held my hand and led us to the car.

Ari and Aria bid us sad farewells before Ari spoke. "Bro, I'll catch up with you in Lucerne. See you in Switzerland in a couple of days. Take care and drive safely."

Looking in my direction, he continued, "Young, take super care of him. He needs your support and love more than ever. Love our dearest brother. See you soon."

On a sad note, we drove toward the direction of Neuschwanstein, Bavaria, our next destination after Vaduz.

———෮෮—

Füssen

Finally, Andy and I arrived at the village of Füssen and checked into the Schlosshotel Lisl (Castle from Lisl hotel), an intimate lodging for a couple in love. Andy was, to say the least, not in the best of moods that day. I did my best to provide him with good cheer along our lengthy journey. I knew full well the difficulties we had with parents, especially when we had to keep secrets regarding our involvements with EROS. Yet Andy and I were glad we had each other in our lives. With the enlightened and supportive advice from our clandestine members, we were able to cope and adjust pretty well to the demands of our teenage lives.

Since our vacation, I finally had Andy to myself, not having to share him with friends or his family. Sitting by the cozy fireplace, we required no dialogue; we were contented to be in each other's company enjoying the peace, tranquility, and joy emanating from our inner beings. Nobody was present to interrupt our blissful happiness and despondent contentment. For the first time since Andy shared my bed, we were blissfully one with each other.

Loving Andy was natural and easy, much like well-oiled equipment churning smoothly as the gears fit together effortlessly. After a light dinner at the hotel restaurant, we retired to our villa for a quiet evening, just the two of us. Seated comfortably in front of the fireplace, I leaned against my lover's chest as he lovingly stroked my hair with his nimble fingers. Feeling his intoxicating breath against the back of my neck, I voluntarily tilted my ear to receive his transcendent breathing, which was decisively stirring my loins to wake. Andy's closeness encased me in an aura of indescribable passion, wrapping me in a cocoon of sensuality as I surrendered willingly to my lover's gentle caresses.

Before long, his sensuous tongue was nibbling at my ear lobes, sending electric currents to my arching spine. As he turned me to him, we kissed longingly, prying each other's lips open as we gave in to our intimate desires. His manliness overwhelms me still. Darting chills of enraptured kisses pleasured my body, tempting me to surrender my nakedness to his alluring masculinity. Slowly but surely, our love dance took flight, inhaling and releasing our life forces into the cores of our inner beings. We were inseparable; we were merging into an undecipherable entity of love.

Pieces of clothing lay discarded on the floor as we moved with sensual precision to our rhythmic love tango. Andy's intoxicating scent held me captive while my unconditional love sealed our union, propelling us into blissful states of transcendent nirvana. The fiery warmth captured by our innumerable body heat took flight as we sealed our earthly bond; we were spiraling upward to meet the heavenly gods of Olympia. My lover needed no lubricant to slide inside me; neither did I require added stimulation to surrender to my handsome Apollo. Lustful orgasmic releases were not required to satisfy our human longings; I was happy to feel his love deep within, and he was utterly delighted to bathe in my glowing warmth. Together we lay in our overflowing nectar of sweet contentment, rocking ourselves into a lullaby of peaceful slumber. I was one with my beloved and he with me. United, we did not wake until the following morning. I didn't want his stiffness to leave, and neither did he desire to release from my core. We stayed entangled until our hungry stomachs called to be fed. We finally disengaged, vowing to be together again as soon as we have an opportunity.

After a delicious breakfast, we rented a horse-drawn sleigh to Neuschwanctein Castle. This fairytale castle had forever been etched into the walls of my childhood room and my unforgettable memories. Now I was on my way to see the original specimen located high above the alpine slopes. My fairytale dream had manifested into reality, but, unfortunately, due to heavy snowfall, our visit was canceled. The treacherous winding roads up the mountain slopes were closed; they were deemed too dangerous to travel.

Instead, Andy and I went round the foothills of Neuschwanctein Castle, en route to King Ludwig II's childhood home: Schloss Hohenschuangau (Hohenschwangau Castle). When my guardian sat snugly with reins in hand, I took the opportunity to discuss the logistics of a triplet relationship between Oscar, him, and me.

Covered in thick blankets of fur, we set off round the mountain with two strong black horses pulling our sleigh. As the horses trotted toward the direction of Hohenschwangau Castle, a wonderful sensation rushed over me. I was transported to the winter scene as portrayed in the famous 1965 *Doctor Zhivago* movie, where Omar Sharif and Julie Christie, wrapped in luxurious furs, rode a similar horse-drawn sleigh on the Russian steps. For a brief moment I also imagined being King Ludwig II of Bavaria on his sleigh, gliding toward Neuschwanctein Castle, toward his fantasy sanctuary.

"I love you," I couldn't help whispering to Andy as our horses trotted away. My beloved smiled, returning a loving gaze in my direction as I continued, "I've been thinking seriously about the triplet relationship you proposed, and I have questions. I need clarifications."

"What do you not understand, my sweet one?" Andy asked.

"Can three people love one another without being jealous of each other?" I asked.

"Well, that depends on how loving and giving the three parties are. You see, Young, in order for this type of relationship to work, each member of the trio must be secure within himself and not feel threatened by one or the other. Oscar, you, and I must love one another unconditionally and contribute our best interest to all within the triangle."

"Can you provide me an example?" I asked.

"Let's take, for instance, our lovemaking last evening. Say I am with you and we are in passionate throes of intimacy, not wanting a third-party involvement. If Oscar loves us unconditionally, he will allow us time alone and not be jealous or demand participation in our love duet unless we invite him into our inner sanctum. Similarly, if I see you and Oscar in the act of passionate lovemaking and if the two of you don't want to be intruded upon, I will retreat without jealousy, knowing full well that the both of you love me nonetheless, but at that particular moment, the two of you want to be alone together. The same applies to you if you witness Oscar and me during our moments of intimacy.

"I understand this can be difficult for us, and one might suffer the feeling of rejection. That is why I stress that the individuals must be secure in themselves in order not to feel threatened by the other two lovers."

Looking adoringly at my valet, I commented, "You are so enlightened and light years ahead in your ideology of love. I wish I could be more like you."

Andy, finding my remark amusing, said, grinning, "My darling Young, you are the sweetest person I've ever met, and I love you because you are you, and I love you no other way. In regards to being more like me, I believe you are doing just fine without imitating my philosophies. You will realize that when you love a person unconditionally, you will automatically open yourself to his happiness. The happier that person or persons are, the more joy will flow into your own life."

"How do you control jealousies?" I was curious to find out my valet's response on this topic.

He laughingly answered, "Young one, jealousy is a choice, like all other choices. You can either change your thought patterns when the green-eyed monster rears its ugly head or let the beast control every fiber of your being. It is up to you to determine if you want to be the victim or the victor.

"Any more questions, my dear?"

I smiled contentedly, keeping quiet until we arrived at the various historical destinations we were visiting that day. One of them was the Museum of the City of Füssen. That day was one of the most pleasant and memorable experiences in my young life. I was coming into my own by just being with Andy.

⚶ EMBRACING THE STORM ⚶

Dorothy Tinker

THE BATTLE had been pointless.

Nay, Tælen amended as he stared out the window of the room he'd rented at the Golden Bones Inn. *The battle wasn't pointless. It earned us sympathy from the king.*

The damage and the pain, however. . . .

Ten ships altogether had taken damage in the attack the king's men had made on the Tauresian pirates. Nearly a third of their alliance. The deaths had been few, thankfully, but the casualties still numbered too high for Tælen's liking.

"Don' tell me we rented this nice room from Jemiah only for you to spen' the night contemplatin' the harbor."

Tælen's lips twitched. He didn't turn away from the window, but it wasn't necessary for him to recognize that the other man was pouting.

"*Don' sulk,*" Voz squawked from her perch on the windowsill. "*It doesn' become you.*"

Tælen frowned and turned his gaze onto the red and blue lora. "*That is not what I wished to say, Voz.*"

The large bird ruffled her feathers and twisted her head around to stare up at him with one eye. "*I do not understand your tastes,*" she crooned instead of repeating the words he'd expected her to speak. "*Sí, the red of his feathers is nice, but his other coverings aren't bright enough.*"

Tælen snorted and glanced over his shoulder finally. *He* was lounging on the large bed the innkeeper's wife had offered them, his head tilted back to show off the tan length of his neck. Tælen followed the curve with his eyes, followed it to his collarbone and the glimpse of taut muscle that his dark-blue tunic revealed.

"*His clothes might not be bright enough for you,*" Tælen finally told Voz in the tongue of the animals, "*but I don't understand your tastes, either. Why don't you leave me to mine?*"

Voz chirruped in surprise, and Tælen could feel her considering his words.

As an Animal Mage, Tælen had magic that allowed him to communicate with, and even control, animals. When he was younger, the magic had kept him sane. Having been born mute, making friends with humans had been nearly impossible, so the magic had allowed him to find companionship among the animals.

When he was nine, he'd proven himself capable enough to be accepted as a deckhand on one of His Majesty's ships, but his lack of speech had made rising through the ranks an impossibility. Even befriending Voz, who gave him the chance to speak his mind to the humans around him, hadn't convinced the ship's officers that he was capable of doing more, so it was little wonder that he had eventually joined the crew of a pirate ship.

"Stop reminiscing," Voz whistled and shook herself. *"Gods, you're in a mood tonight. Maybe you should join with your mate."*

Tælen glanced back at the bed. *"He's not my life mate,"* he answered, but the sight of his lover's thick, red braid snaking over the bed beside his lithe form stole the strength from his words.

"Didn't say he was, did I?" Voz admonished. Turning her body to face out the window, she cast Tælen a final glance and murmured a soft *"You don't have to be life-bonded to be devoted,"* and launched herself into the night sky.

Tælen watched her red and blue form disappear into the night before finally turning away from the window. Voz was right about one thing, at least: he'd spent long enough contemplating the past.

—⁓—

Dayphin laid his head back with a sigh. Tælen had been so silent since the council meeting ended. Not that the captain of the Silent Raider could actually speak, but he had taken to staring into the distance and not responding physically to Dayphin's words.

And I think Voz might be taking advantage with what she says. Tælen would never have said that about sulking not becoming me.

He frowned, considering the way he'd worded that thought, and then grimaced. *Although, I guess I have been awfully sulky today.*

It was simply that Dayphin was accustomed to spending his free time at port with Tælen, and while he'd spent the afternoon on Tælen's ship, they'd been too busy dealing with the aftermath from the soldiers' attacks to actually spend much time together. Unlike Dayphin's Wind Runner, the Silent Raider had been the victim of the first battle fire, an attack that had landed too close to Tælen for Dayphin's liking.

The redhead was musing over the injuries that Tælen had finally had a Mage Healer take a look at when a touch to his knee made him blink and lift his head. Tælen leaned over the foot of the bed, one hand firmly planted beside Dayphin's right knee, the other hovering steadily over Dayphin's left thigh. As soon as Dayphin met Tælen's gaze, the brown-haired captain quirked a smile and let his hovering fingers settle lightly just above Dayphin's knee.

Dayphin caught his breath at the touch. It was a gentle touch, almost too gentle for him to feel through the cloth of his trousers, but it was enough for Dayphin to imagine the feel of those fingers on his bare skin.

As he watched, unable to look away, Tælen glided his fingers slowly up Dayphin's thigh. At first, they eased over the top of his thigh, dancing gently over the swell of muscle, but as they passed the midway point, they curved around to the side until they came to rest at the edge of his hip.

"Damn it," Dayphin hissed when Tælen didn't move for nearly a minute. Dropping his head back down to the bed, Dayphin tried to slow his already erratic breathing. "Don' tease me, Tæ."

A huff of breath against the center of Dayphin's chest startled a soft groan from the young pirate captain, and Dayphin tilted his head down to find Tælen leaning over him, his body less than a hand above the redhead's, his eyes crinkled warmly.

"What—?" Dayphin began, but then he stopped as he realized that he hadn't heard a squawk, chirrup, whistle, rustle of feathers, or any other sign that Voz was nearby for several minutes. Darting his eyes around the room, he confirmed that he and Tælen were truly alone before meeting the older captain's eyes once more.

"But your voice . . ."

Dayphin trailed off as Tælen raised one eyebrow and smirked. Heat flooded Dayphin's cheeks. Nay, Tælen didn't need Voz to make Dayphin understand him. His eyes, lips, and fingers were fluent enough.

And his tongue, Dayphin amended with a gasp a moment later as Tælen drew a thin, wet line from the middle of Dayphin's chest, where the gap of his tunic ended, up to the hollow of his throat. There, Tælen nibbled at the skin, and the nip of his teeth sent shocks through the base of Dayphin's spine.

"Tæ . . ."

Tælen's teeth paused just long enough for him to smirk against Dayphin's throat before he dragged his lips up to the side of Dayphin's neck and began to suck. The redhead grunted. His lover's lips were high enough that Dayphin knew all of his men would be able to see the mark the next day, but the pressure felt too good for him to care.

As Tælen sucked, he slid his fingers up under the edge of Dayphin's tunic. Calloused fingertips ran up Dayphin's side, and the redhead dug his teeth into his bottom lip, holding back the cry that tried to escape.

Unfortunately, it escaped anyway when a sharp tug on his hair jerked his head to the right, exposing the line of his throat for a more thorough exploration by Tælen's teeth. The touch of Tælen's slick tongue between sharp nips drew whimpers from Dayphin, and he finally closed his eyes so he could lose himself to the sensations of Tælen working over him.

—⁓—

Tælen pulled back to admire the bruises forming across Dayphin's throat. He didn't usually like to leave marks where his lover's men could see them and use them as an excuse to tease the redhead. Tonight, however, he felt a pressing need to claim the man in a way that others couldn't doubt.

You don't have to be life-bonded to be devoted. Voz's words echoed through his mind, but he shook his head and slid one hand under Dayphin's neck, urging him upright.

Moments later they were both stripped of their tunics, and Dayphin's golden-brown gaze, just visible in the lamplight, roved hungrily over Tælen's chest. Unable to prevent a smirk from pulling at his lips, the silent captain dropped his own gaze.

The younger man, much to Tælen's continuous delight, was all lightly tanned skin and mutinous freckles. It was a state that Dayphin both cursed and took pride in, but Tælen had always appreciated the beautiful dance the freckles made across the redhead's skin.

Especially here.

Lifting a hand to follow his gaze, Tælen lightly traced the path of a particular trail of freckles. The small brown spots darted from the high edge of Dayphin's collarbone across to his left shoulder and then dipped down the curve of his chest, curling almost lovingly around his left nipple. As Tælen's fingers skittered along the trail, just brushing the edge of puckered skin, Dayphin gasped.

"Please, Tæ," he whispered. "More."

Lifting his gaze back to Dayphin's, Tælen lowered his head and flicked his tongue across the puckered nipple. The groan that broke from Dayphin's throat urged Tælen forward, and he closed his lips around the small nub.

Whimpers broke over him as fingers dug into his shoulders, and Tælen slid his hands down Dayphin's back, cupped his buttocks, and hauled the younger man into his lap.

The sudden press of arousals, even clothed, was enough to still them both, and Tælen took a shaky breath to prevent himself from simply throwing the red-head back onto the bed and finishing this sooner than either of them would have liked. Instead, once he was certain he could control himself, he dug fingers into the top of Dayphin's thick braid and dragged him down into a press of lips and tongues and teeth.

Dayphin pressed himself into Tælen as fully as possible: mouth to mouth, chest to chest, manhood to manhood. Only the tug and pull of large hands on his buttocks and head made him waver as the urge to press into Tælen's grip rivaled the need to meet his frontal assault.

But meet it he did. Dayphin might like the feel of Tælen claiming him, but he was still a pirate, and a captain to boot. He had never been one to back down from a challenge, and the scrape of Tælen's trimmed beard across his smooth chin was as much a challenge as the soldiers' attacks on the Silent Raider earlier in the day had been.

Dayphin hissed sharply as thoughts of just how much he could have lost in the soldiers' assault suddenly threatened to drown him. It was all too easy to recall his first sight of Tælen and Voz after the battle—both covered in soot and Tælen injured—and twist the image in his mind until all he could see was Tælen's broken body among the wreckage of the Silent Raider. He knew the ship had survived mostly intact and that Tælen, by some miracle, had lost none of his men.

But he also remembered Voz's unease when she'd informed him of just how close that first battle fire had come to killing the man they both loved.

Gentle fingers traced his jaw then, startling Dayphin. Lifting his eyes, he blinked as Tælen's face swam into focus, and the silent man dragged a thumb beneath one eye and then the other, collecting the tears as they fell.

"Tæ . . ." Dayphin whispered, but the older man shook his head. Tracing his fingers along Dayphin's jaw once more, he leaned forward and pressed his lips gently to Dayphin's. The redhead took a shaky breath as his lover slid his lips back and forth, and warm pressure swelled within Dayphin's chest.

"I . . ."

The pressure was too much for Dayphin to speak around, and he closed his eyes and gave himself up to the gentle caress of lips against his own and fingers slipping along his chin and throat and into his hair. Even then, his lover's touch remained light and his calloused fingers were soon soothing down Dayphin's spine before brushing teasingly along the edge of his trousers.

Dayphin nodded as the teasing touches continued, answering the silent request to go further. As the fingers dipped beneath fabric though, Dayphin sobbed and broke away from the kiss, burying his face in the crook of Tælen's neck. The older man hesitated, his fingers slipping back up Dayphin's back, but the redhead shook his head and clutched at Tælen's sides.

"Nay! I want—"

A soft "hush" startled the redhead into silence as Tælen wrapped his strong arms around Dayphin's thin frame. Dayphin shivered. This was what he loved about Tælen. The man was strong, confident, and indomitable, yet he also bore such gentleness that Dayphin knew he would never hurt him.

At least not intentionally.

The thought pulled another sob from Dayphin's throat, and he pressed his face harder into the side of Tælen's neck. "I don't . . ." he gasped. "I can't . . ."

Tælen shushed him again, but Dayphin shook his head. "Nay, I have to. I nearly lost you today, Tæ. I can't . . ."

The silent captain's arms tightened around Dayphin's body, and the redhead relaxed into the embrace willingly. "I don't know what I would do if I could never see you, feel you." Dayphin shivered and said, "I don't know what I would do if I lost you forever."

You don't have to be life-bonded to be devoted.

The words reverberated through Tælen's mind once more, but this time he couldn't bring himself to ignore them. He had denied Voz's claim that Dayphin was his mate, but they had been lovers for nearly five years now. It had begun with simple passion, but Dayphin's words were proof that Tælen wasn't the only one who had considered the implications of the day's battle.

And what it might mean for us.

"Tæ?" Dayphin whispered, his face still pressed to Tælen's neck. Tælen tilted his head and stroked the back of his lover's head. Dayphin sighed and rubbed his face back and forth before murmuring, "I want to forget today. I don't want to consider that I might—"

The redhead's breath caught, but Tælen didn't need him to finish to understand what he wanted. Lifting his chin, he brushed a light kiss upon his lips and then lowered him to the bed.

—∿∿—

Dayphin felt like a ship floating on a calm sea. Tælen's hands were gentle as they moved over him, slipping the boots from his feet and his trousers down his legs. When they turned him over and smoothed over his back, a sigh left his lips and he buried his face into the pillow of his arms.

The scent of herbs touched his nose just before Tælen's fingers slid between his thighs, and he spread his legs, wanting the pleasure those questing digits promised. When they pressed against his opening, he bit his lip for only a moment before he forced himself to relax, and the first finger slid inside with ease.

One finger became two, which were soon joined by a third, and the sea Dayphin floated upon grew stormier. But it was a storm he knew and craved, and he panted and pressed back against the fingers that filled him. The fingers shook briefly before continuing to slide within him, and Dayphin lifted his head to glare over his shoulder, certain that Tælen was laughing at him.

When he met the older man's eyes though, they were darkened nearly to black and so intense that Dayphin had to remind himself to breathe as he squirmed beneath his lover's heavy gaze and light touch.

It wasn't much longer before Dayphin's sea was tossing him from wave to wave, and he cried out, demanding that Tælen move on before Dayphin chose to ignore him in favor of his own hand. A sudden *smack* accompanied a flare of heat on the redhead's left buttock, but the pleasure that followed as Tælen removed his fingers and replaced them with the length Dayphin craved was worth the small flash of pain.

After that, the storm filled Dayphin completely. Lightning flashed up and down his spine. Thunder shook him, stern to bow. Wind even whipped across his back as Tælen joined him at sea, and they not only weathered the storm, but embraced it.

——⁓——

Tælen stared down at the sleeping redhead. His body felt heavy, and his eyes ached, but his mind refused to let him rest. He couldn't, not when the day could have ended so very differently.

If the soldiers' attack had hit the deck just a little closer to me, or if the assault had begun against Dayphin's ship instead of mine. . . .

Tælen took a shaky breath and closed his eyes. His hands shook, but he couldn't get them to stop, not when thoughts of what could have happened circled through his mind like sharks gathering at the scent of blood.

"I thought your mood was supposed to improve when you joined with your mate."

Tælen blinked and turned toward the window, where the soft whistle had come from. Voz stood on the sill, her form silhouetted against the lights of the docks.

"Usually, aye," Tælen replied when he realized she was expecting an answer.

"So?" she chirruped. Launching herself from the windowsill, she flew to the end of the bed and peered at the sleeping redhead. *"Why are you still so maudlin?"*

Tælen grimaced and turned his gaze back to Dayphin. *"I could have died, Voz, as you've been so quick to point out. Maur's Blood, if those particular soldiers had been farther down the dock . . ."*

He shook his head. *"We're pirates. There's always been a risk of death. Aye, it's been better since Marlen created the Pact and we pledged our allegiance to the Evonese throne, but today only proved that death still looms over us. And we—"*

"Nonsense!" Voz trilled, though she kept the sound soft enough not to wake Dayphin. *"You're both alive. You should be celebrating that."*

"How can we though? The danger just became more obvious."

Voz shook herself, fluffing up her feathers, and then nudged Tælen's arm with her beak. *"You may not be able to remove the danger, but you can make a promise: One that will withstand the danger. Or at the very least, weather the storm."*

"And embrace it," Tælen replied, remembering the words Dayphin had whispered before he'd fallen asleep.

Voz bobbed her head. *"Indeed,"* she whistled.

Tælen glanced around the room. *"If I'm going to make him such a promise, I need a ring."*

The lora twisted her head behind her back, dug her beak into her feathers, and carefully plucked one out. Turning back to Tælen, she offered it to her silent captain. *"A piece of your voice."*

Tælen bowed his head and accepted the feather, which gleamed a bright blue even in the lamplight. *"Are you sure?"*

"Like I would let you make a promise to him without my help," the lora trilled in response. *"I may not understand your tastes, but that doesn't mean I don't like them."*

Tælen nodded and turned back to the sleeping Dayphin. After a moment of searching the bed, he smiled and lifted his hand, trailing the long, red strand of hair he'd found. *"Now all I need is something to represent what brings us together."*

Voz trilled and launched herself back toward the window. *"Leave that to me."*

—⁓—

Dayphin stretched, sighing happily. It had been too long since he and Tælen had last indulged in each other, and last night's activities had ensured that he slept well.

"Good morning."

Dayphin grinned, not bothering to open his eyes. "G'mornin' to you too, Tælen. I see you got your voice back."

"Aye."

Dayphin started and blinked open his eyes. Voz had sounded much closer than he had expected that last time. When he could finally focus, he found himself staring directly at the red and blue lora, who appeared to be holding something out to him in one claw.

"Wha's this?" he muttered, plucking the item from her claw and tilting it so he could get a better look. It was round and covered in red and blue.

Dayphin stilled as he realized what he was holding. Lifting his gaze, he sought Tælen's. "What?"

Tælen met his eyes and smiled warmly, a sight that warmed Dayphin's belly and chest and made him bite his lip. *"Wanted to make you a promise,"* Voz whistled. *"And ask a question too."*

Dayphin sat up and stared down at the ring he held. The red and blue he had noticed was the red of his own hair and the blue of Voz's feathers, but the actual ring itself. . . .

"Is this—?"

"*Sea stone,*" Voz answered. She sounded so proud that Dayphin glanced at her with narrowed eyes. "*Voz found it,*" she added, lifting her beak. "*Not telling how, though.*"

Dayphin blinked and frowned down at the ring. He couldn't imagine how the lora had managed to find a stone worn down by the sea to be a perfect ring, not to mention. . . .

Dayphin slid the ring onto the second finger on his dominant hand. Sure enough, it was a perfect fit.

"*Not telling,*" Voz repeated.

Dayphin took a shaky breath and stared at the ring. *What does it matter how she found it? What matters is why.*

Lifting his head to meet Tælen's gaze once more, he whispered, "Aye. The answer is aye."

Taelen broke into a grin. Before Dayphin realized what was happening, the older man was hauling from the bed into a hug that crushed him against his chest and made it difficult to breathe.

Dayphin didn't care, though. He and Tælen would life-bond, and then they would be life mates for the rest of their lives. Wrapping his arms around Tælen in return, Dayphin buried his face against the older man's chest and inhaled deeply.

Together, we'll not only weather the storms of life, but embrace them.

⤳ JESCAPADE ⤳

Erika Small

JESS WAS EXCITED to embark on this new chapter of her life. As the only child born to parents with highly profiled careers, she was no stranger to receiving lots of attention. Standing 6'2" with an athletic build envied by most, she wasn't a stranger to random stares and looks of confusion from strangers either. So as she prepared to walk into the offices of Logenboth, Tandler, and Vasher for the first time, she was confident and well prepared for whatever was to come. She was told that the eyes of all would be on her because she was so heavily recruited as the new director of safety operations for the company's Fleet Management Division. This new position meant a move for Jess. She was a country girl from a somewhat small town, and though she had traveled with her parents over the years, this move to the big city was somewhat of a big deal for her.

Jess had been attracted to women for as long as she could remember. One of the jokes she told to describe how she knew she was a lesbian included a detailed description of the dreams she had of her first-grade teacher and of one day proposing to the beautiful, curvy redhead. Jess hadn't engaged in many relationships over the years. She had mainly focused on her education and directed all of her energy to achieving high career goals.

Jess's parents never really accepted her sexual preference. They were never shy to share their thoughts that she would one day grow out of that phase, find a wonderful man, marry, and make them grandparents. Jess always secretly believed the least she could do would be to become extremely successful since she wasn't planning on ever making them grandparents.

As Jess proceeded through the revolving doors and headed for the elevators, she felt the eyes of many passersby, some going so far as to point in her direction as they shared conversation with the individuals they were gathered with. She received just as many, maybe more, smiles and nods of approval, which warmed her insides and eased the mild anxiety she had about her new experience. She entered the elevator, pressed the number thirteen, and stood silently as the elevator announced each floor as it stopped.

As she exited the elevator and approached the large contemporary receptionist desk, the mildly attractive young lady behind the desk said, "You must be Jessica Morris."

Jess confirmed her assumption and asked how she knew. The receptionist explained that it was way too early for visitors and she was accustomed to seeing the same faces exit the elevators every day. Cyndi, the receptionist, introduced herself and Jess quickly expressed her desire to be called Jess instead of Jessica, citing the only people who called her by her full name were her parents. Cyndi kindly corrected and graciously led Jess to the boardroom where she was scheduled to report. As she left Jess in the boardroom, she said she would notify her superiors that Jess had arrived.

As Jess waited, standing and looking out the window at the view of the city, she couldn't help but smile. She had arrived. Her life was shaping up to be everything she desired. About a month prior, she had acquired her dream loft with the help of an agent recommended by her new employer. The company vehicle assigned to her for all of her transportation needs just happened to be a series above the one she had looked into purchasing back home. To top it off, she was hours away from completing her first day at her dream job. For the first time, Jess found herself thinking, *If only I had someone to share this all with.* But, she didn't. It was just her: Jess and her career. So it was time to take it on and dedicate 200% to becoming the best director of safety operations that Logenboth, Tandler, and Vasher had ever seen. One by one, the mostly male team began to file into the boardroom, all seemingly extremely excited to meet Jess. It was apparent Cyndi had notified everyone of the name preference because not a one of them called her Jessica.

That's until Bethany walked in.

As Bethany Stork entered the room, it was as if there was no other sound than the movement of her luxurious red hair as it whisked from one side to the other of her broad yet extremely feminine shoulders atop her well-curved 5'9"frame. It was as if the first-grade teacher who appeared in all of those childhood dreams had appeared in the flesh. As Jess returned from her temperately paralyzing stupor, she was still being handed down compliments on her achievements as a student, of assessment results received and being showered with gratitude for joining the team. As Bethany approached Jess, she quickly said, "Jessica Morris, I've heard nothing but exceptional things about you."

"Thank you, ma'am," Jess replied. "And everybody calls me Jess."

"Everybody?" Bethany questioned.

"Well, everyone here I should say."

"Well, I never have been just like everyone here so I might as well not start today. If it's okay with you, I'll stick with Jessica. It just feels better."

"Well of course, if it feels better, I wouldn't have it any other way!"

The two shared a quick stare then parted ways as everyone made their way to their seats as others continued to file into the room.

———✳———

The meeting was pretty much a brief introduction of Jess to the rest of the executive staff. She was given everyone's name, title, and how they would be beneficial in her new role. Jess quickly began to feel as though she was an important part of the team. Jess was definitely all about the business. However, she couldn't help from time to time, glancing across the long boardroom table at the beautiful Bethany Stork. Bethany caught one of her glances, and the two shared a smile. As the meeting was nearing its close, George Tandler, COO, asked who would be willing to show Jess to her poorly located shabbily decorated office. Bethany quickly rose to the occasion.

George gave the thumbs up, looked at Jess with a cheeky grin, and said, "I'm sure you'll just hate it!"

As the two walked down the hall, Bethany pointed out a few of the offices along the way and explained that she had taken the long route to show her the most important of all.

"If you ever need anything at all, this is where you can find me probably more than I'm willing to admit." She smirked and then said, "It's what has landed me my position though, so I'll take it."

The two shared a few more moments of staring, both with seductive smiles, before they headed just down the hall to Jess's new office. Once they arrived, Jess gazed over the large, obviously newly decorated office with windows wall to wall overlooking the city. She turned to Bethany and said, "Wow—I think George is right: I'm simply gonna hate this place."

Bethany reached and patted Jess on the forearm and said, "Enjoy your new home, Jessica!" She then headed back down the hall, but not before making Jess promise to let her know if she needed help with anything. As Jess sat reclined in her nice, comfy new office chair, she gazed out of the window, taking time to reflect and enjoy her new adventure. Just as she was doing so, one of her new colleagues entered her office and told her that in case she didn't get the memo, the executive masquerade party was in a couple months and she would surely be expected to be in attendance. He assured her it was enough time for her to acquire an outfit and even a hot date if she chose to. Jess thanked him for the info and went on with arranging her new office.

She thought about all of the hard work she had put in to get there and immediately became thankful for and wanted to call her parents. So she did. When Jess's mom answered the phone, she quickly exclaimed, "I knew this had to be you calling from this strange area code! How's my baby doing?"

"I'm wonderful, mom," Jess replied with a sigh. "Still trying to take it all in!"

"I know it's beautiful," her mom added.

"It is mom. You guys have to come visit soon!" she said. "Where's dad?"

"He's in this house somewhere. You know your father. Let me call him."

As she waited for her husband to enter the room, Jess's mom began to ask questions about everything Jess had already experienced.

"Well that sounds good, baby," she said as she handed the phone to Jess's father.

"Hey there, sweetie!" he exclaimed. "Tell me all about it."

As Jess shared the happenings with her father, she for some reason felt the need to share with him that there was one other woman on the team and her name was Bethany Stork. She thought about why she had done that for a brief second, before her father interrupted the thought by saying, "I haven't heard you say anything about finding or even looking for a church to attend."

Jess sighed and said to her dad, "You're right dad, I haven't yet, but that is definitely on the top of my agenda."

"That's good to hear," he replied before they exchanged a few more pleasantries and released the line.

The rest of Jess's first day on the job was pretty uneventful. She returned to her new plush loft, gathered her things for the following day, and prepared for bed. As she showered that evening, she couldn't help thinking of Bethany. She wondered if she were single and what her story was. As she drifted off to sleep, her dreams continued with the same thoughts. She dreamed of Bethany entering her office, closing and locking the door, neither saying a word, and them beginning to engage in a make-out session steamier than anything she had ever encountered in real life. She woke up in a cold sweat that morning. Her dreams did nothing more than fuel her desire to know more about Bethany and what she was about.

As she entered the building the next morning, she opted to take the scenic route, the route Bethany had chosen the previous day to show her where her office was. As she approached Bethany's office, her heart began to race, thinking of the dream she had the night before. Once crossing the doorway, there she was. She was even more beautiful than Jess remembered the day before.

"Good morning, Bethany." Jess said.

"Well good morning, Jessica. How are you this morning?" Bethany returned.

"I'm doing well. Ready to get a jump-start on the day. And you?"

"I am as well," Bethany said with a cute smirk.

"Just trying to recover from not getting much sleep last night. I kept having the oddest dreams," Bethany said as she glanced at Jess with seductive eyes.

This caught Jess off guard, and she stumbled over her words as she said, "Really? Anything you want to share?"

"No," Bethany said. "I should probably keep them to myself."

"Well, I hope you're able to focus today," Jess said, wondering if she possibly could have had dreams similar to the one she had the night before.

Bethany looked at her with a smile and said, "Thank you Jessica. I appreciate that. I'm sure I'll be able to get myself together once I've had a cup of coffee or so."

Jess smiled and proceeded to walk to her office when Bethany called her back to ask if she would be attending the executive masquerade party. Jess told her she had not yet acquired an outfit or a date but she would definitely be there. Bethany told her not to worry and assured her she wouldn't be the only person there without a date and that most executives attended without their significant others. Jess thought this would be the perfect time to ask Bethany if she were single, but she passed on the opportunity. She didn't want to seem pushy or inappropriate, even though she was sure the vibe she was receiving from Bethany was not imagined.

"Thanks for the heads up," Jess said as she quickly whisked away toward her office.

When Jess arrived, she had a visitor waiting there for her. Carter Winston III, a junior executive for the company, was sitting in one of the chairs adjacent to Jess's desk, obviously awaiting her arrival. He seemed overjoyed when he saw Jess walk in. He quickly asked Jess to forgive him for the early-morning intrusion but explained that he was eager to meet her before he began his day.

Eager he was for sure. The more Jess listened to Carter, the more she realized he had no real business with her other than to make her acquaintance. Jess told Carter how appreciative she was that he stopped by and attempted to coast him out of her office, but not before he was able to invite her to attend his church. This caught Jess off guard. She wasn't at all accustomed to being approached about anything having to do with religion in a professional setting. She hesitated and then quickly remembered the conversation she had with her father the night before. She asked Carter if he wouldn't mind writing down the information for her and told him she just might take him up on the invitation on the upcoming Sunday. Carter gladly gave her the information and beamed from ear to ear as he told her of the weekly service they were having that evening. He mentioned that he wasn't sure what she was used to but that she would be in for a treat. Jess thanked him again and took a seat in her office chair as if to signal to Carter that she was ready for him to go.

Once alone, Jess immediately began researching information for the project she was given the day before. This consumed the remainder of the day, and she didn't have time to think of anything else. When Jess was comfortable and felt she had accomplished an adequate amount of research for the day, she gathered her things and headed for her car. During the ride, Jess began to think of outfit selections for the upcoming masquerade party. She decided to visit the local mall to see what she could find.

Once in the area, she noticed a familiar street name. She pulled the info sheet Carter had given her and saw that the church was located on this street. She looked at the time and thought she might as well check it out. After all, Carter had assured her she would enjoy it. She had a whole week to find the perfect outfit. Her dad would be proud.

As she drove into the parking lot of the dome-like building, she didn't know what to expect. It seemed massive. Once inside, she saw it was exactly that: a huge building with what seemed like hundreds in attendance. The service was nice. It was a bit more than Jess was used to but was still nice.

As she filed in line to exit the building, she heard a mild, somewhat angelic voice say "Hi there. Is this your first time here?"

Jess looked slightly to her left to see if the question she heard was directed at her. Indeed it was. What she saw gave her instant butterflies. An absolutely stunning woman was on the other end of those words. Jess was no stranger to beautiful women. However, it seemed as if the women in the big city seemed to have an edge on the small-town beauties she was used to. And so far from what she could tell, they were not nearly as reserved.

Even though Jess was sure the young woman as talking to her, she pointed to herself and asked, "Me?"

"Yes, you." the lady said.

"Oh. Yes it is," Jess replied.

"Well, hello. My name is Sandy. And you are?"

"I'm Jess," she replied. "Jess Morris. Nice to meet you."

"Likewise," Sandy said with an innocent yet sneakily seductive smile.

The two stood in silence for a few moments before Sandy welcomed her and asked what brought her there that evening. After explaining that she was new to town and was invited by a colleague, Sandy seemed even more excited and went on to tell Jess that she was glad she decided to come out. She mentioned that if Jess was single, they had a singles group that went out from time to time. If Jess wanted, Sandy would give her the info. Jess told her yes and thanked her.

Sandy looked in her bag as if she were searching for literature and then quickly turned to Jess and said, "It doesn't seem as though I have the brochure with me. Why don't you give me your number and I can call you with the info?" Jess thought this a bit forward but didn't let that stop her from giving Sandy her number. They exchanged smiles. "Awesome. I'll be in touch," Sandy said.

"I'll look forward to it," Jess replied. As she walked away, Jess wondered if the exchange was truly as sensual as it felt to her or if Sandy's beauty had simply taken her to another place. She was determined to not allow it to consume her as she headed home to prepare for the next day.

The next few days went over without incident. Jess did find herself thinking a few times that she must have imagined what she felt was chemistry between herself and Sandy. She had sporadic thoughts of visiting Bethany's office to see if the drawing power she felt between them was still there. Instead she decided to delve into her project to ensure it was the best it could be.

Suddenly her office phone rang. Cyndi, announced she had a Sandy Thomas on the line asking to speak with her. Jess hurriedly told Cyndi to patch her through.

"This is Jess," she said, attempting to sound unruffled.

Sandy went on to explain who she was and apologized for contacting her at work. She said that she had somehow lost Jess's number and remembered Jess telling her where she worked, so Sandy hoped it would be OK that she reached out. Jess assured her there was no apology needed and told her she was glad to hear from her. Sandy promptly stated that Jess should join her for lunch if she truly meant what she said. Jess swiftly accepted, and they discussed the details. Once off the phone, Jess sat for a spell reflecting on the conversation and felt a sense of fulfillment. Maybe it was time for her to love. After all, she had everything else she ever wanted, and it was obvious she was correct in believing she and Sandy had a connection.

—⁓—

Lunch was great. During the time they shared, Sandy and Jess discovered many similarities. It was as if it were meant to be. The two planned on having dinner the following evening, which they did, and many dates were to follow. The two were nearly inseparable. Jess found herself completely smitten with Sandy. So much so that she invited her to the upcoming executive masquerade ball. Jess still found herself thinking of Bethany from time to time. The two still shared glances and smirks when passing one another in the hall or in the elevator. However, her time spent with Sandy had been so consistent that she was sure Sandy was who she should be with. She never truly liked the idea of an office romance, anyway.

—⁓—

The night of the masquerade party, the executive floor was nearly empty. It was obvious everyone had taken off to prepare for the evening. Jess called Sandy to confirm their meeting arrangements and headed out for the evening herself. As she walked down the hall she ran into Bethany, looking as beautiful as ever. It was apparent Bethany was in a hurry to get out of the office, as she simply told Jess she looked forward to seeing her that evening and rushed for the elevator. Jess returned the sentiment, all along thinking maybe she should have told her she was going to have a date for the evening. She retracted those thoughts, considering the only romantic exchange the two had shared was in the comforts of her head.

—⁓—

The ball was held at the most exclusive hotel in the city. Jess had visited some nice places but didn't mind sharing with Sandy that this hotel possessed amenities she was not at all accustomed to. The two of them were having and amazing time that evening. Logenboth, Tandler, and Vasher was not shy about providing their executives with the best. This, of course, included the best premium alcohol there was to offer, and it was plentiful. Jess and Sandy joked with one another about not knowing exactly how much they had to drink for the evening. Neither was worried about driving because the company had provided suites for all of the executives for the evening.

Jess introduced Sandy to executive after executive. She was excited to have her as her date. As she was sharing conversation with one of the few wives in the room, Jess excused herself to the ladies room. As she walked in, she saw Bethany standing in the mirror attempting to adjust her dress.

"There you are," Jess said. "I was wondering why I hadn't seen you this evening."

"Well, I'm having a slight wardrobe malfunction," Bethany explained.

"Anything I can help you with?" Jess asked.

"If you could help me with this zipper, I would be indebted to you forever," Bethany said with a look of desperation.

"Sure thing," Jess said. As she stepped closer, Bethany's scent took over her senses. She rubbed Bethany's shoulder and told her how good she smelled.

"Really?" Bethany asked. "How good?"

"I would say good enough to eat," Jess said, toying.

Bethany turned to Jess, and before either could give it a second thought, they began to share the most passionate kiss either could have ever imagined. It seemed as though when either of the two attempted to pull away, the passion would increase, emoting even more affection. Before long, Jess found herself removing the dress Bethany had just asked her to help zip up. They explored every inch of each other's body with both their hands and lips without a second thought. As they climaxed together, it was as if they were kindred spirits. At that very moment, nothing at all was wrong with their connection. It was then Jess thought about Sandy. She offered to help Bethany back into her dress, attempted to make herself presentable, and exited the lounge-styled ladies' room without uttering another word. As she exited she saw Sandy approaching.

"I thought you had gotten lost," Sandy said with a smile.

"No. I just needed a minute," Jess said.

"Is everything OK?" Sandy asked.

"Yes," Jess said. "Let's just get back to the party."

"I'm having an amazing time," Sandy said with a schoolgirl grin. "Thank you for bringing me, babe! I love you!"

"I love you too, babe," Jess responded with a forced smile and an extreme feeling of guilt.

As the two returned to the party, Jess grabbed another cocktail in an effort to forget what had just transpired. Not only had she just shared a passionate exchange with Bethany, but she and Sandy had exchanged the "L" word for the first time. She was nearly overcome with emotions internally.

As if that weren't enough to deal with in one moment, Sandy leaned in to her and whispered, "I can't wait to get you upstairs. Do you think it's OK that we say goodnight to everyone?"

Jess thought to be a good idea, hoping that if they retreated to their suite soon enough she might be able to avoid running into Bethany. Then the unthinkable happened.

"Bethany!" Sandy suddenly exclaimed in a seemingly excited tone. Jess's heart dropped. It was as if she was in that same paralyzing stupor as when she had seen Bethany for the first time. As luck would have it, Bethany and Sandy shared a mutual friend whose parties they had both attended in the past.

"Sandy!" Bethany said in just as an excited tone. That was until she could clearly see there was some sort of connection between Jess and Sandy. "It's great to see you, Sandy. Who are you here with?" she asked, secretly praying Sandy wouldn't say what had become obvious by the look on Jess's face.

As Sandy explained to Bethany that she and Jess had been dating for some time, Bethany began to look ill. When Sandy asked her if she was OK, she quickly told her she was and explained that she thought she might have had too much to drink on an empty stomach. The excused herself abruptly and disappeared out of the ballroom doors. Jess was left there feeling somewhat ill herself. Sandy was none the wiser and was just determined to head upstairs and consummate the love she and Jess had just proclaimed.

Jess said her goodbyes to her colleagues and thanked them for a lovely evening. Sandy couldn't seem to keep her hands off her. As she and Jess entered the elevator, she began to unbutton Jess's shirt, caress her breasts, and kiss her with what seemed like everything she had to offer. Once they reached the room, she was ready to go all the way. Jess tried with all her might to give her as much passion as she had exuded just moments ago with Bethany, but it just wasn't there.

Sandy was still none the wiser. To her, she and Jess had reached a level in their relationship that was at the point of no return. As Sandy drifted off to sleep, Jess lay beside her thinking of the events of the evening. She fought the urge to call Bethany, fearing the exchange would be more than either could bare. She wanted to ensure her that the passion they experienced was real. Instead she remained in bed next to Sandy feeling that what they had shared could only be described as a mediocre session.

Jess did have genuine feelings for Sandy. The time they had spent together over the past couple of months had proven to be like nothing she had ever experienced before. However, it didn't hold a candle to what she experienced with Bethany in the ladies' lounge of the ritzy hotel. Jess was confused. She didn't know if she should just blow off her encounter with Bethany as a night of passion. Or was there something there? Could it be possible that she and Bethany could share the passion they had, along with enjoying time with one another as she and Sandy did?

Would Bethany even be willing to give it a try? Office romances hardly ever turned out well. Was this going to have an effect on their business relationship? All these things ran through Jess's mind as she watched Sandy sleep beside her. And then the biggest of all: What if Sandy found out about her escapade with Bethany? That would kill her.

The two shared a close, mutual friend. It was sure to come out. Was it something she should disclose herself? Surely that wasn't the answer. That would never go over well. Maybe she could talk to Bethany and plead with her to not disclose the events and express that she never intended things go that way.

So many things clogged Jess's mind that night that she was unable to sleep a wink. Sandy woke up the next morning revived and sounding as though she was ready to start planning their future. Jess felt that they were moving extremely fast, but while hanging onto the guilt from the evening, she just allowed Sandy to say what she liked, and Jess agreed with it all. After all, Sandy was a nice girl. She possessed all the qualities in a partner that Jess had always wanted. Who's to say that the passion shared between her and Bethany wasn't a fluke? She had decided she wasn't willing to risk it and knew that meant she would have to have a conversation with Bethany.

Jess pondered over what she would actually say for the remainder of the weekend. She decided a text or even a phone call would not be sufficient and knew it would have to be face to face. She walked into Bethany's office that Monday morning confident she had all the right words. As she entered, an extremely tall handsome gentleman stood near the doorway.

"Is Bethany around?" she asked.

"She'll be shortly. Feel free to wait," he said as he extended his hand. "Jim. Jim Stork, Bethany's husband. And you are?"

Jess chuckled both inside and out as she extended her hand. "Jess Morris. Very pleased to meet you, sir!"

Jess walked away with an extreme feeling of relief. All the grief she had given herself over the weekend was unwarranted, at least where Bethany was concerned. And to think, she pondered giving up what she had with Sandy for Bethany, not knowing all along that Bethany was just another Jesscapade.

CINNAMON WITH A DASH OF SUBURBAN DESPERATION

Elizabeth Ann Domino

IT STARTS INNOCENTLY ENOUGH: a stolen glance here and there while in the carpool line at 4 p.m. A minute glance as she waters the azaleas on Sundays and I scrape paint off the siding. Maybe it's the way her jeans cling to her supple ass or the way her breasts strain against the sheer top. Maybe it's the way the wind blows ever so slightly, and if I strain hard enough I can make out the outline of a nipple. I almost fall off the ladder that day.

When she glances my way, her doe-shaped cinnamon eyes burn into me and I wonder if she suspects the nasty things I want to do to her.

Who knows? What I do know is the Saturday I saw her at Simon's soccer game in a pink dress bending over to reach for a Gatorade, I knew I was in trouble. I went home that afternoon and locked myself in the bathroom while everyone met for pizza at Luigi's, and I masturbated until I thought my hand would go numb.

Just the thought of her plump quivering lips and her round tits bouncing in my face is enough to send me into a whirlwind. Day and night, all I can think about was her.

I begin to time my drop-off and pickup of the kids just to coincide with her dropping off Ian. With every volunteer opportunity that comes my way, I am there, giddy like a pubescent fourteen-year-old.

Then comes the weekend of the Daddy-Daughter dance, and I take off from work to volunteer in the gym with setup on Friday. I walk into a fuchsia sea of helium balloons and taffeta to find her swishing through a crowd of glaring, jealous, pimple-pocked freshman and I almost cream in my pants.

My heart begins to pound, and I back into the nearest bleacher as she lengthens her stride toward me. A moment of silence passes, and she introduces herself formally and reaches to shake my hand. The fact that she has to remind me who she is even though we have been neighbors since I downsized into the house down the street leaves me embarrassed and in awe.

I can't tell you what her name is even if I was listening, because it doesn't matter. Not when I envision the way her thigh met her inner groin and picture my face buried within it.

Christ! What was I doing? I hadn't even looked at someone else since the divorce, and the ensuing shuffle from one house to the other and two Christmases had put a damper on any sex drive I thought had survived.

Until now. When she takes my hand and tells me we need to run to her house to pick up some more crepe paper, the palm I return is drenched in sweat. She giggles as she wipes her hand on her jeans.

Next thing I know, we cross the hot asphalt and escape the glaring sun as we climb into her Tahoe, and I can feel my temperature boil as she leans across me to buckle my belt because obviously I am useless.

She leans in a little close as she draws back, and I feel her flick her tongue against my left ear lobe and sigh.

Her eyes meet mine, and within four minutes we are turning down Brindle Lane and into a driveway of a home bearing a pristine, picturesque white picket fence.

I can barely process what I can only imagine will follow. Then I register to the fact she is already half way across the lawn. She throws her hair over her shoulder and gestures with a slight jerk of her head and coyly smirks before bouncing onto the stoop.

I scramble in my haste to exit the vehicle and almost pay for it with a busted lip and chipped tooth. Regaining my composure, I take my time weaving my way past the perfectly manicured flowerbeds and onto the porch, where a large ornate brass door stands between me and the fantasies that have consumed me for months.

As I enter the darkened house, I hear the beating of my heart as I cross the threshold, and I feel a hand pull me into the shadows.

The shadows brought about my undoing. As we spend more and more time together, I realize the desperation in my kisses, the loneliness in my hands, the quickness with which she drops to her knees as our afternoon trysts increase. And I wonder if I have made a fatal mistake, until that simple sound breaks my thoughts and I find myself succumbing to her seduction.

"Shhh . . ." her voice trails with a soulful huskiness.

The slow hiss of the whisper slides off her tongue, and my heart flutters with anticipation as she shoves me back onto the bed. The darkened room casts shadows against the buttery sheets, and I feel the warmth of her breath, the mist of the air tickle across my cheek.

I turn my face toward her lips and her tongue shoots in and out, clamoring for a chance to find its way into mine—and she does. Our tongues entwine and dart in and out as I feel her hand slipping above my head. The jerk of my arms being pinned to the headboard sends shivers down my spine.

Her other hand glides down my silhouette until it finds its way to my hip, where it lingers as she licks my clavicle. My throat catches and she's back. I can taste the honey of her lips as she bites my lower lip.

I panic, and my eyes dart toward the clock on the table: 1 p.m. A wave of calm settles over me, if only for a moment. Her hand resumes its exploration, and as I feel her teeth sink into my tongue, her fingers set my body on fire.

The undulating cadence of their rhythm quickens with every gasp I heave, and I find myself sinking deeper and deeper into the sheets. The moistness of her lips lingers for but a second before her mouth traces the same path her hand has already so expertly traveled.

Stopping intermittently for a sharp bite or suckling, I feel her mouth envelope my nipple whole and I cry out. I glance down and find the silky ebony curtains part and the cinnamon pools of her iris glowing in the dark. She stops suddenly, and I see her bend over the edge of the bed.

In a flurry, my hands are now clasped above my head with silk restraints, freeing her to intrude every curve of my body. One hand clasps my breast as the other slows its gait before it too joins in kneading my flesh.

I am drowning and cannot catch my breath as beads of sweat trickle down my back. She shifts her hands to my hips and I find her drawing them closer and closer into her. I feel the tip of her tongue following the circle of my navel, and she lets out a low-pitched hum as she blows out across my pelvic bone.

One last glance with those glowing embers and she ducks, spreading my legs gently with her palm, and buries herself deep inside me. With every flick of her tongue into my slit, I am driven into a state of sheer madness as I find myself bucking harder and faster against my restraints.

I scream out in frustration and yank harder, at last freeing myself from the knots she so painstakingly tied in preparation for this day. Or maybe she does this for all the girls.

I jerk my knees and raise them to her shoulders as I simultaneously position my hips higher. I grab the long locks of her mane and shove her deep within my sex and hold on as we reach that final crescendo. As quickly as she left, she has now found her way back to my lips.

The taste of our mingled scent is salty and thick. I quickly flip her on her back. Now the aggressor, I straddle her hips as I pull her into a sitting position and we begin to sway, her mouth now swallowing the spreading blush of my left nipple into the soft folds of her mouth.

I arch my back and feel the tangles of my hair sweeping across the small of my back. I feel it coming back, and the intense fire that engulfed my body just moments ago is now returning. It is joined by heat—the sweat I feel pouring off her skin.

We sway and rock, fighting against the impending tick tock I see out of the corner of my eye and the screech of the familiar 3 p.m. bus on the corner.

The sounds of our screams are silenced by the trickle of laughter, and we collapse on the bed, a sight of tangled arms and legs akimbo, ragged gasps filling the silence of the house, floating past the PTA budget left unfinished on the counter and the cookies cooling on the rack. The reality of our existence hits us.

This is where we lie until our children descend the steps and bring the flood of homework, teachers' notes, and sack lunches into the house, and the moment is lost.

And then she will take her casserole dish I borrowed and the signup sheet for carpool and make her way slowly down the sidewalk, those cinnamon orbs casting a longing glance from four houses down: the one with the pristine, picturesque white picket fence.

And I will sit. And wait. In a silent, empty house with peeling paint. For a husband who never returns and a life I never once lived.

.

DESIRED BY DEFAULT

Thomas Kearnes

THERE WAS A PATH, and no one could see it but me. Each time Cutter and I went to the bathhouse, I shot through the halls of rented rooms, past the bank of grimy, oblong windows overlooking the outdoor pool, through the steam room, and beside the hot tub. I needed to be numb. Cutter so enjoyed all the flesh on display. I couldn't refuse him. Occasionally, of course, I found a man to bring back to our room, but honestly, I would've been happy had Cutter been the only man beside me, loving me. Even with him near, I needed the tweak to keep me from stripping away my skin. Every time, part of me considered scrambling home, and every time, the rest of me remained paralyzed with desire. I could never leave our rented room.

Cutter and I sat on his bed, passing the pipe. Posters of great Greek landmarks covered his walls. A twittering blue jay outside his window distracted him, so I snuck another hit.

"Careful, boy." His gaze didn't leave the window. "Don't get so high you can't get hard."

I grinned, delighted to be caught. Cutter always found me out. Perhaps that was a condition of love. "Why do you think I'm always the catcher?"

"'Cause you like what I pitch."

I laughed and passed the pipe. Cutter was good to me. He volunteered his house in uptown Dallas for our weekends and occasional weeknights together. I still lived in a dorm with a nosy kid from the East Coast.

True, Cutter was thirty-seven, but I did my best not to think what would happen, how that age gap would bend and flex into something more obscene if we managed to stay together after these first few months. When he reached fifty, I would be thirty-three. These weekly trips to the Dallas Spa were the price of admission, I told myself, the cost of procuring a boyfriend as accomplished, sexy, and—well—manly as Cutter Drake.

"Just a few more hits," I said. "You know, to fortify me."

"You and your big words."

"I'm sorry, but that place . . . you know."

He scooped the long end of the pipe into the tiny plastic bag of tweak and ushered another rock into its mouth. "Yes, Darren. I'm aware of your feelings about the bathhouse."

My boyfriend was gorgeous, and I wasn't his only admirer. At the bathhouse, I watched the way men never stopped but turned their heads, keeping their eyes on Cutter as he passed. He had a fantastic body. He liked to call me from the twenty-four-hour gym downtown to brag whenever he maxed more weight while working out. But it was his face—the way his smile spread like melting butter— that was where I caught myself gazing whenever he was distracted. The slim, sharp nose, the pale-gray eyes, the long locks of rust-colored hair that flopped past his eyebrows. And best of all, he was a *man*—masculine and confident, not like those prissy, shaven boys trolling the sidewalks in Oak Lawn.

"I'm sorry." I meant it, but it didn't sound like I did.

"We don't have to go," he said.

"You love it there."

"I love watching men fuck you."

I tried to smile. Granted, Cutter never forced any man on me. I got final approval on each trick. Always, at some point, as Cutter took snapshots with his smartphone, I began to drift. I thought about Cutter invading me after the stranger left, what he would say, how he would praise me, like a beloved pet. I did these things, these men, for *him*. Whenever I broke away from an encounter to look at him, however, I saw the pride, the lust in his eyes. I assured myself there was no higher calling than pleasing the man who loved you.

"It'll be past four when we get there," I said. "We'll be hours ahead of the club crowd."

"Too many twinks at night. The guys in the afternoon are *men*."

"Like you," I said.

He pulled me close and kissed me so softly, I felt my heart drop into my stomach. The blue jay twittered again outside. I listened to its panicked cries as Cutter eased me down onto the bed. He set the pipe on the nightstand and eased his frame upon me. Perhaps we wouldn't make the bathhouse till five, six, or later!

—◊◊◊—

Cutter carried an old black gym bag to the bathhouse. Inside were all the necessities for fucking strangers: lubricant, condoms, bottles of Gatorade, cock rings, a tweak pipe, and about an eight-ball of clear crystals. We strolled down Swiss Avenue staring straight ahead.

Our first time there, Cutter had warned me it was considered impolite to make eye contact with men leaving the building. Frank appraisal only occurred in the halls, among the labyrinth of numbered rooms. Or, sometimes in the steam room and sauna. Basically, anywhere beyond the check-in desk was fair game. At the time, it didn't make sense, but I did as instructed, not acknowledging the gaze of a passing muscle guy.

Today, there was no one leaving when we arrived. Cutter joked with the skinny man behind the check-in counter. He flashed his credit card and then collected our room key and the threadbare white towels. We wore them after shedding our clothes. Our check-in complete, Cutter grandly swung out his arm to catch the swinging door. I chuckled at his mock chivalry.

We strolled through the lounge. It was very large, a pool table at one end and, at the other, an arrangement of couches and chairs before a big-screen television. Cutter once told me the men who frequented this room were either too ugly for sex or too wired to chase it. A Cameron Diaz movie played to the small group of bare-chested men seated around the set. My gaze fell on one of them. He was maybe forty with a solid build. Coarse chest hair partially obscured his admirable physique. He swiveled his head, catching me as I stared. I averted my gaze, but Cutter noted our awkward exchange.

"Already on the prowl, boy?"

"No, I just, I thought I knew him."

"Probably saw him here before."

"I'm sure that's it." I forced my voice up an octave, like a stewardess instructing passengers how to save their own damn lives. I asked if he'd rented the VIP room.

"Follow me and see where I go." Cutter grabbed my wrist, pulling me through the curved hallway that connected the lounge to the halls of rented rooms. We passed the stone archway leading to the hot tub, showers, and sauna. Cutter insisted I shower after sex, no matter how brief the encounter. Built into the stone hallway was a series of windows looking out over the kidney-shaped pool and stone sundeck. It was an overcast autumn day; no men occupied the deck chairs. As we entered the first hall, the awful staccato of electronic house music thumped over the speakers. I never understood gay men remixing perfectly good songs until one sounded like the next. In my intoxicated state, though, I found the steady bass soothing. I imagined Cutter penetrating me in time to the pulsing beat.

He led me down a small hallway with no doors on either side. He'd booked the VIP room after all! There were only three such rooms in the club, each complete with a queen-size sheeted mattress, pillows, and a television bolted high on the wall, playing nonstop gay pornography. There was plenty of room to maneuver and play, unlike the regular rooms, which were the size of broom closets, the twin-size rubber mattress taking up half the space.

While thrilled with our swank accommodations, a prick of fear settled at the base of my skull. Why shell out the cash for a VIP room unless he planned something exotic, something that did not arouse me. Various unpleasant scenarios flitted through my head. Cutter tossed his gym bag on the bed and began to strip.

"Hurry up and get undressed. We've gotta get your ass plowed."

I tried to laugh but instead produced a strange, sticky sound. Within minutes some strange man would ram his shaft inside me, and I suddenly felt tired and slow, like expired gelatin. I didn't want to be here. I wasn't sure where I wanted to be, instead, but my anxiety needed no specific locale.

"Been working out more?" Cutter glanced at my naked torso.

I shrugged, smiling shyly. At the moment, I couldn't remember whether I had.

"Your abs are getting more defined. Keep up the good work," he commented.

I rubbed my taut abdomen, doubting his praise. Cutter, towel wrapped around his waist, pulled me into an embrace. "You're a very sexy boy, Darren Young." He said it with such burnt-ember huskiness that I knew I'd consent to whatever he desired. I had friends who yearned for such grand compliments. I knew I was lucky. My luck had its own presence apart from us.

"You should find someone in no time," Cutter whispered into my ear.

I wrapped the towel around my waist. I was tempted to haggle for a little more tweak, but I didn't want to delay. He put such effort into these trips. In reality, my role was incidental.

I felt foolish, so I left the room. As instructed, I left the door cracked open so any passing man could glimpse Cutter stroking himself. After rotating my shoulders to loosen up, I looked both ways down the hall, wondering which way was best. One led back the maze's entrance, the other into the depths. I had yet to pass any man, so I ventured further into the maze. The high floodlights dimmed as I ambled forward, the hallway finally opening into a wider hall, this one with closed doors, on each side, all in a row. Actually, not every door was shut. I passed one room and saw inside a young black man pleasuring himself, watching himself masturbate with stern concentration. He never noticed me. Cutter and I had an agreement: white men only.

A moment later, a young couple passed, their heads tilted together as if they exchanged military code. They were my age, and one of them—the brunet— was scalding hot: a lithe, long body, mouth like an open cut in the skin. Both glanced at me, and I noted their haughtiness, these members of the Dallas Gay Mafia. You ran into these men everywhere in the Oak Lawn, the city's gay nexus. They dressed impeccably, with gym-toned bodies and beautiful, unblemished faces. They condemned anyone less fantastic with a sneer, including me. I wasn't unattractive. I studied myself in the mirror before every visit to the bathhouse, as if my looks might have soured overnight. These Mafia boys could make any man feel instantly worthless. I looked away. One laughed as they passed me. His boyfriend half-heartedly shushed him before laughing himself. I admired their brazen belief in their power to attract.

When searching for men, I simply circled the hallways until finding one. Men left rooms, returned from the showers or elsewhere, as a steady tide of new faces. I noticed an older man, maybe forty-five, with a beer belly and graying fur matted on his shoulders. Next I saw a scrawny Mexican kid who flashed me a gold-toothed smile that I adamantly ignored. There was a trio of men, each around thirty, in a heated, hushed discussion, none of them gazing at me even when my arm brushed one of theirs. How long would I circle these halls? Some days it could take fifteen minutes. Had anyone knocked on the door of our VIP room, taking the open door as an invite? He might now be pounding some guy senseless. I didn't want to be here. I tried my luck elsewhere.

The hot tub was a brown-tiled in-ground pool with rushing jets protruding from its walls, roiling the water, often just lukewarm. Today offered no surprise. I slipped off my towel and entered the water.

There were three other men in the pool, but my eyes locked on just one. He sat at the opposite end, absently waving his arms through the bubbles. He was perhaps thirty, with long, dirty blond hair hanging past his jawline. A wide, welcoming smile seemed in response to a private joke. I felt awkward staring so long, but the man finally broke from his reverie and met my gaze. My God, such a smile!

"You're cute," I said. Excessive wit was just wasted breath.

"So are you."

I moved closer, the warm water thick around my hips and thighs. The man let me come closer. "You been partying?" I asked.

"Maybe. You got some more?"

"I never come without it." The gravity of that statement spooked me.

"Is it just you here? You come with a friend?"

"My boyfriend, Cutter," I replied.

"I wanna know *your* name." The man hesitantly pressed his palm against my chest.

"Darren," I said.

"So, your boyfriend likes threesomes?"

"Actually, he like to watch hot guys fuck me."

His smile never faded, but his eyes narrowed. "What does he do while I'm pounding you?"

"He takes pictures."

A doubtful expression appeared. "You mean, for a website?"

"Oh, no, no, no. Just for our personal use." Then I volunteered something I hadn't planned: "I think he jacks off to them when I'm not around."

His head snapped back, a gasp of amusement wrenched loose. I hadn't believed it that funny, but I laughed too. When he laughed, whoever he was, you laughed with him.

"We're staying in one of the VIP rooms," I said. "You ever been inside one?"

"A few months ago." He smiled earnestly. I felt cheap. "Hope I live up to your boyfriend's expectations."

"You'll like Cutter. He just enjoys the show."

He told me his name was Raymond. I'd forgotten to ask. As we made our way to the VIP room, not speaking, I wondered how long I could've gone with knowing what to call him. I found the door still cracked. I eased it farther open. Cutter had dimmed the lights, so it took me a moment to make out his figure, him stroking himself while onscreen moans filled the room.

"Looks like he may be busy," Raymond muttered.

"He's was waiting," I replied, equally quiet. Then, louder, I called out, "I brought company!"

Cutter bolted upright and smiled. Whether it was meant exclusively for me, I couldn't tell.

Cutter rose from the bed and asked him if I'd informed our guest of our situation. He didn't bother with the towel. He extended his hand to Raymond.

"Didn't tell me how hot you'd be," Raymond replied.

"I'm not the main attraction."

"Where should we start?" Raymond blithely tossed his white towel onto the stone floor.

"Kiss him for now," my boyfriend instructed. "Move slowly."

Raymond theatrically slapped his hands together. He then slid them around my waist and gently pulled me into his arms. "I can go slow," he murmured, more for me than Cutter.

He kissed me. Every time a new man kissed me, I compared his kiss to Cutter's. The strangers' kisses were rarely better, but Raymond knew how to flutter his thick, plump lips effortlessly over my mouth. After a few moments, the tip of his tongue pushed its way through my lips. I allowed it entry. Our kiss deepened.

Cutter watched in silence. As my head teetered back and forth under the force of the kiss, I caught a brief glance at my boyfriend. He stood motionless, his smartphone loosely held. This was unusual. Typically Cutter couldn't wait to start shooting. Worry distracted me from Raymond's commanding kiss, but he didn't seem to notice. Cutter snapped out of his daze and aimed the phone. He snapped several shots in a row, never changing position. Raymond's hands grew bolder. The towel remained snug around my hips. Through the fabric, Raymond's desire couldn't be ignored.

"Darren," Cutter called, his voice soft. Raymond wouldn't stop kissing me.

"What?" I asked, breathless.

"Suck his cock."

"Now?"

"Yeah, man. I wanna see that shit right *now*."

"Sounds good." Raymond added in a softer voice. "If that's all right with you, buddy."

Raymond was a handsome man. His face had yet to register the smile lines and slight crow's feet that Cutter's face held. There was a slight gap between his two front teeth. He instinctively bowed his head whenever he smiled. His eyes were a dazzling cornflower blue.

"Sure," I replied, easing down to my knees. I slid him between my lips, allowing him to surge all the way to the back of my throat. My head bobbed, oddly in sync with the onscreen moans. Raymond's moans joined them, filling the room.

"Good boy," muttered Cutter, raising the smartphone to his face. "That's a good boy."

Raymond tasted fantastic. I felt the wild charge I always felt knowing I could bring a man that intense a pleasure. You could go mad with the power. And there was my boyfriend, the man I loved, clicking away with his phone.

I recalled the first time Cutter showed me the photos of a bathhouse encounter. He sequenced them out upon the bedspread, beaming like a proud father. "You look hot in that one, boy," he said. And then, "I thought he was going to scream when you moved your ass like that." And then, "I'm gonna have to watch you close, or you'll run off to the porn studio."

I felt nothing looking at these graphic images. Because of the tweak, I rarely remembered performing these acts, but I played along, pantomiming bashfulness or pride, whatever reaction Cutter wanted. I knew, for him, this part was just as important as the sex itself, if not more so. He urged me to keep a snapshot or two, but I always refused. These were for him, I said. He believed me.

Back in the VIP room, while Raymond gently thrust his hips, sending himself deeper down my throat, I heard a man wail in the distance. I thought it had to be the porn, but this sounded more like a cry of anguish. Also, it definitely came from just outside the closed door. Neither Raymond nor Cutter made any expression to indicate they'd heard it too, so I resumed my task. But then the same cry, only louder.

"What the fuck was that?" Cutter asked.

We heard it again, this time trailing off into a series of jagged sobs.

Even Raymond broke from his bliss. "Is some guy out there crying?"

I stopped sucking and turned to the door. Cutter crossed the room, opening it. From my position on the floor, I couldn't see what the other two saw. But then, a young man staggered through the doorway and dropped to his knees before us. His thin, bony shoulders shook and his arms enveloped his narrow chest. His face contorted in bereavement. While Cutter stood still in front of him, our intruder sobbed and sobbed.

Finally, Raymond spoke. "Dude, what the fuck happened?"

The crying man tried to speak, but no words came. Milky snot ran from his nose and over his lips, glistening in the dim light. He tried to speak again.

Cutter gently placed a hand on his shoulder. "Are you here with someone?" he asked, showing a compassion that surprised me, though I don't know why. Cutter was had shown me kindness countless times. I didn't want to be here. "Can we get you something?"

The man settled down, sank onto the floor, bottom resting on the soles of his feet. He wore only a white towel around his hips. Just like us, I thought. He might be just like us.

"I'm with Jerry," he moaned.

"Is that your boyfriend?" Cutter asked.

"I don't think so," the man stammered. "At least, not anymore!" He began to howl. I tore my gaze away from the wreckage to check on Raymond. His features had darkened, his once-ample mouth shut tightly, the lips thin and severe. He glared at the poor man through slit eyelids. His arms folded tightly over his chest. I turned back to Cutter and the crying man as he tried to help the man to his feet.

"Let's go find Jerry," Cutter said.

"He doesn't want me anymore."

"I'm sure that's not true. C'mon. Let's go."

"No! No! It *is* true! He found some piece of ass at the hot tub! Goodbye, Keith!" His hand fluttered away from him as if trying to escape.

"That's your name?" Cutter asked. "Keith?"

Keith moaned and nodded. H rubbed furiously at his eyes. By then, Cutter had maneuvered the intruder back toward the doorway. Believing the situation almost contained, I returned my attention to Raymond, but he was grabbing his towel from the floor. The brisk strokes he made wrapping it around his waist unnerved me. Only minutes ago, we'd been kissing like long-time lovers, like Cutter and I might.

"You don't have to leave," I said.

"Sorry, man, that was kind of a buzzkill."

Raymond stomped through the door. Cutter and the crying man had already gone outside. I stood there, helpless. I wondered if any of Cutter's snapshots were angled to capture Raymond's lovely face. More likely, they were focused solely on my lips gliding back and forth upon his shaft. That's what my boyfriend wanted to remember: how I looked giving another man pleasure.

The door clicked shut. I glanced down and saw my swollen excitement begin its retreat beneath my towel. This flood of disappointment surprised me. There were other candidates stalking the halls right. All I had to do was wait for Cutter and then leave to find him. When the pursuit reached its fever pitch, I let myself get carried away on the adrenaline.

Still, I needed something to numb myself further, to guarantee no doubts would descend. I hurried to the side of the bed and opened Cutter's gym bag.

I riffled through it, looking for the bag of tweak. Just a couple of hits, that's all I needed. After locating the pipe wrapped inside a sock, I loaded it with a sizable crystal only to realize I'd yet to locate a lighter. I ransacked the bag once again but had no luck. He worried about how much I smoked. Defeated, I sank onto the bed and listlessly watched the screen as one man penetrated another man. I couldn't help wondering whether Raymond and I would have moved with comparable precision.

After a few moments I slid off the bed, slipped the loaded pipe back into the gym bag, and made my way for the door. Even though being alone in the VIP room meant I was spared the glares of the strange men lurking outside, it also meant I had no distraction from the rot and doom I felt in this dank fuck factory.

Just a month ago, I'd spent the night with a man I met while at my cousin's wedding in Tyler. He was big and charming and insatiable. I forgot, at least for a few moments, that Cutter was in Dallas, waiting for me. What if Cutter asked me to do something I simply couldn't stomach? Would he leave me stranded with damp sheets and faded semen stains on the walls?

"My God, some people are so fucking needy!" Cutter burst through the door. He crossed the room a long, energetic stride.

"Did you ever find his boyfriend?"

"I asked his room number, but the guy flat-out refused to go back. You won't believe what happened next." The two men in the porn increased their volume and urgency. Cutter shook his head and smacked his palm against his forehead. "Anyway, we're standing near the hot tub and he grabs my junk, says he want to fuck. We could rent a separate room, his treat."

"Oh my God," I said. It was always painful to be reminded of this: Cutter was a devastatingly gorgeous man. Of course other men desired him. And there was no guarantee they'd desire me too.

"I just looked at him and said—and you should've heard how I said it. I looked him dead in the eye and said, 'I have a boyfriend, you dumb faggot.'"

Making that declaration, he sounded like a no-nonsense sheriff from an old sitcom. I didn't fight the warmth I felt spreading through me after he said that.

"What did he say?" I rose to my knees on the bed.

"He just shrugged, shook his head, and said, 'Your loss.' I guess he's still looking for dick."

"What a loser!" I cried.

"No shit. Maybe we shouldn't have come here today."

I couldn't keep the enthusiasm out of my tone. "You mean you're ready to leave?"

Cutter rounded the bed and stopped. I was still on my knees atop the mattress, so our heads were level. He caressed my cheek. He held my gaze for so long, I forgot about Raymond's electric blue eyes. Yes, there were other desirable men in the world, in this very building, but Cutter Drake had chosen me. *Me.* Whatever I had to endure to keep his love would be endured—enjoyed!

—–∿∿–—

I was exhausted and sweating like a sow in the mid-August sun. I lay beside him, the sheets askew from our thrashing. I listened to Cutter's breath, slowed mine till it felt into rhythm with his. It took me a bit to realize he'd spoken.

"You wanna run outside and grab me a water?" he asked.

"Don't you have Gatorade in your bag?"

"Yeah, but water sounds better."

"I'm so fucking whipped right now," I moaned.

"I'll suck your dick," Cutter said.

I rose to my side and looked at him, hoping he could see my merriment. "You should do that because you love me."

"I'll love you more when I'm hydrated."

I carried a limp dollar in my fist for the drink machine. More than anything, I wished I could make the trek to the lobby without passing any other man. I was done with men for that day—every man except Cutter. I turned the corner and headed out of the maze.

I only saw two men in the hot tub and another three watching the lounge television as I hurried past. None of them noticed me. I slid the dollar into the drink machine and pushed the correct button. Just as I bent over to retrieve the jettisoned bottle, a figure in a white towel materialized beside me.

"You better be grateful he loves you."

Alarmed, I swiftly glanced over my shoulder and saw Keith glaring at me. His eyes were still red and bleary.

"What did you say to me?"

"You heard me the first time."

I gulped. "Cutter told me what you did."

Keith's stance softened. He hitched up one shoulder in defiance. "You know how hot he is; you're the one he's taking home."

"I have to get back to the room," I stammered, abruptly turning to leave. Keith followed me, his wide strides matching my own. I didn't want to be here.

"You think some kid can keep him happy for long?"

"Stop following me!" One of the men watching television turned to see the commotion.

"If he really wanted just you, he wouldn't bring you here."

"I don't wanna talk to you," I insisted.

We had reached the windowed hallway connecting the lounge to the maze. Keith seized my shoulder and spun me around. I couldn't remember the last time a man looked at me with such hate, and I knew he wished me dead. My only crime was being loved and returning that love.

"I'm not giving up, kid," he said. "Men like him get bored with little boys. Remember that."

I nodded dumbly and backed away. I bumped into a wrought-iron table and jumped at the screech the table leg made dragging the floor. Recovering, I ran into the maze, fully expecting Keith to follow. But when I reached the hallway leading to our VIP room, he was gone. Taking a moment to collect myself before joining Cutter—I couldn't tell him about this, never!—I felt hot, tears stinging the corners of my eyes. I pawed at them, ashamed. Taking a deep breath, I turned the doorknob.

"What took you so long, boy?"

"There was more than one brand of water," I said.

"That's bullshit. I don't care what the label says; water is fucking water."

I handed him the drink. He grabbed it and unscrewed the lid. Knowing I was giving myself away, I stared at my boyfriend as if trying to memorize his face before he vanished among these rented rooms and rented desires.

"Boy, what's wrong?"

"Please, let's go home!"

I felt the tears slide down my cheeks. I buried my face in my hands. The shakes my body made as I cried left no doubt that I needed my man to comfort me—right now.

Cutter embraced me. "Baby, it's all right. I didn't know this place upset you that much."

"It does; it does."

He tried to laugh. "C'mon, boy, you're not supposed to cry in a bathhouse."

"What *can* you do here?"

My boyfriend, the man I loved, smiled. "This," he said and pressed his mouth over mine. With that, I was silenced. Through the speakers, an insistent bass line pounded. The boys on television groaned and grunted. Cutter pulled his face away. He gazed into my eyes. Did he want me to do something? I couldn't remember the last time I'd seen that look, so I simply smiled, awaiting his next desire.

✦ BY FORCE IF NECESSARY ✦

Thomas Kearnes

WHEN A MAN TUMBLES into bed with me, an absurd hope churns. It's like indigestion. Louis and I have been kissing and sighing since we met at the bar. We lusted our way west on the interstate. I'm flattered he agreed to drive so far out of his way. He offers me some tweak, but I tell him it would interfere with my sainthood.

He shucks his clothes so fast that I haven't time to be aroused. I prefer to slowly strip a man, discover his body like an exotic destination. He makes no move to help me undress. I'm too drunk for disappointment to register. Once I'm naked, Louis instructs me to lie prone on the bed. Determined to keep smiling, I explain that I like to watch a man while he fucks me. Louis chuckles and assures me there's nothing I'd want to see. I'm a sucker for self-deprecation.

Height and build similar to mine, Louis positions his body atop my back and penetrates me. Throughout our fuck, he moves nothing but his hips. He mumbles into my ear, but there's no point in listening. I've been with his kind: they hit autopilot the moment we hit the sheets. It's best to find a spot on the wall and visit my happy place.

He drills me with deadening rhythm. He must think Texas crude resides inside my ass. I keep trying, foolishly, to decipher his low-register grunts. When the intensity of his moans escalates, I relax a bit. I look forward to his orgasm more than he does.

If that fucking college boy hadn't dumped me last year, none of this would be happening. I cross Louis's name off my mental list: two exes down, four more to go.

—◦∿◦—

Put enough tweak up your nose, I believed, and an erection was an erection. That night at the house, an agreeable ranch-style residence located too far off the road for neighbors to hear a scream, I sat in Hayden's lap. We passed the pipe between us. It turned me on to watch those big, billowy meth clouds.

I was young enough to find any man's advances flattering. Surely, I thought, we'd follow our usual pattern: He'd flirt with me, the aggression slowly increasing, until I made a lame excuse and left the room. That night, however, he pulled me back upon his lap when I tried to leave. I laughed and tried again to stand. I couldn't conceive that another man might consider me his due, willing to seize it if he must. Fortunately, his attack was clumsy, hands always a moment too late. I fled to the opposite side of the room, the door ajar beside me. I savored my victory. No one raped Jared Glidewell!

I informed him that he was dead to me. This last conversation was, indeed, our last. If he so much as waved hello, I'd tell every fag in East Texas not only that he was a premature ejaculator but also that he had the virus. I kept the attack secret. If I admitted being spun when attacked, those fags would've slammed me swift like God.

—⁓—

I always have better luck at the Longview bars than the one in Tyler. The atmosphere is more relaxed, and gossip hasn't been elevated to a blood sport. I never get loaded enough to wipe out on the interstate. Besides, when a funny, curly-haired cutie like this one follows me home, turning him down is a mortal sin. True, he isn't on the list, but restricting my sex life to that goddamn college boy's exes seems needlessly Spartan.

His clothes slip from his frame as I lock the front door. His eyes are kind. Why haven't I noticed until now? There's something subtly comforting about him. Sometimes tricking with a strange dude leaves you paralyzed, unsure how to execute even simple social rituals. Never mind that, he's kissing me and doing it well. He whispers for me to lie prone on the bed so we can make love. It's so rare to find a guy who doesn't call it *fucking*, if he calls it anything.

He's on top, his hips in motion, but the rest of him remains still. Typically I like men to be more creative, but when he has lips this soft and teasing, I can overlook it. I don't need my happy place. This cute guy asks again if my name is Jared. Sure, I say. It hasn't changed since he asked me at the club. My failure to remember his name, I hope, would remain my secret.

"I think we've hung out before," he says, hips never breaking rhythm.

"I don't remember you," I say.

"Please don't tell my ego."

"Did we meet before I switched apartments?" A busted pipe flooded my place last spring, sending me to the complex across the street. Several of my tricks knocked at my old address only to find a generic crazy cat lady.

"Last year, I think."

I wrench my neck to glance at the man on my back. At least he *seems* pleased to encounter me again. "Oh, yeah! If I'd seen you in my old bedroom," I assure him, "I would've remembered. My new curtains threw me."

"You ever run into Doug, like at the club or online?"

True, I'm on a mission to fuck every last one of that dickhead college boy's ex-boyfriends. True, I have only two more left. Actually, just one if I include Louis. Don't interpret that to mean, however, that I harbor any interest in seeing my ex again. His restraining order against me smacks of melodrama.

Before I answer his question, Louis ducks into the bathroom for a quick snort. It's dangerous, I know, to expose myself to these situations. I won't attempt to explain. I have a vision for my life, and right now, Louis improves the view. His rote sexual technique needs help and needed it yesterday, but snobbery dilutes the scattered and disconnected gay population of East Texas. Loneliness is never by choice. Louis still in the toilet, I fetch a beer.

I've never fucked a guy for a second time while thinking it was the first. Of course, I wouldn't know if I had. There's nothing left to do but cross off his name again. I never anticipated that I might like one of these clowns. I take a long gulp.

I didn't know what Lucille was thinking when she showed me her story. I didn't think she read short pieces, unless assigned.

While still in my twenties, I fantasized about writing movies. I imagined myself climbing the stage to accept my Oscar, thanking an assortment of celebrities for making this moment possible. Hell, I would've thanked Lucille, too. Six months as an unpaid reader for a no-name production company cured me of that delusion. Self-expression led to disappointment, both in yourself and in those you love.

Lucille's story recounted an evening just before Christmas when she and some childhood friends followed a trio of Goths back to their apartment for a party. One of them quickly swooped in and forced her to do many awful things. It was odd. Discovering proof of a friend's vulnerability should have made her more human, more worthy of compassion, but I thought only of the damage. She was the retarded sister hell-bent on forcing love and joy down your gullet.

She asked me what I thought. Be honest, she said. I can take it, she said. Pausing, I established eye contact and leaned in. She could help so many rape survivors, I said. She blushed, tears in her eyes. We embraced. It's true that she might help other women, but her story wasn't worth a damn. I didn't lie about art. She became a dietician.

—◦◦◦—

For the moment, I've abandoned my mission. The last ex on my list is studying art history in New England. It never struck me that hunting Doug's past boyfriends might include airfare. Of course, I haven't told Louis about my mission. In fact, I've mentioned little about my time with Doug, my ex. Louis, though, has told me plenty about the kid. He's nice, Louis confides, but *needs* a man, desperately. Tugging me toward the bed, he tells me every great romance collapses the instant someone hails its greatness.

Louis has proven just as inflexible in the bedroom as his initial performances suggested. When I propose new positions, he asks if I'm still having fun. The glassiness in his eyes and slackness of his mouth, however, hint that he isn't too interested in my answer. Spooning me after we satisfy one another, Louis breath catches. I've been matching my breaths to his and chill to hear myself exhaling alone. Finally he props himself up on his pillow, body stretched beside mine. I hope he won't ask me to get high. We've had that conversation too many times. I wish he didn't have to snort before we drifted toward assignation.

"I've always wanted to try something," he says, "but I never trusted the guy enough."

I smile. "You trust me?"

"Not one hundred percent." He laughs.

"We're gay men, Louie. There aren't many taboos left to explore."

"Have you ever been raped?" he asks.

His tone is so neutral, as if asking for a match, that it takes a moment to process the question. We can't return to the push and plow of our first time. It's my turn to stop breathing.

Louis shrugs and flutters his hand. "I'm sorry. It's terrible. I shouldn't—"

"I had a close call seven or eight years ago."

"Here in Tyler?" Louis asks.

"Just ten minutes away." I turn to gauge his reaction and gaze as his expression tightens.

"Here it is," he says. "Every time we fuck, I want you to *violate* me."

"Louis, I've had friends go through this shit. It's a nightmare." I look at him. He has no idea how appalling his request sounds. "I'll think about it this week." I stroke his arm. "It's quite a detour."

His warm smile flickers. I haven't told him, but a familiar number appeared on my cell phone sometime last night. Five calls over two hours and no messages. I don't understand. How could I respond with the restraining order in effect? Doug hasn't forgotten that. I imagine him pumping Louis' buttocks, Louis crying out in terror.

—⁂—

Not long before third grade, Mom and I were having a quiet dinner at Luby's. She never liked cooking. The friendly man appeared at our table, asking Mom how she'd been, inquiring why my father wasn't with us, and I didn't know how to act. Mom and Dad's main rules for interactions with their friends were to be polite, don't intrude, and always mention my stellar grades.

I thought my father was invincible. Each time he left town to protect a judge or jury, I pictured him pulling his piece on some husky-voiced bad guy. I thought it was noble wanting to save the day. Not realistic, but noble.

The friendly man joined us for dinner and paid for the dinner. Mom smiled throughout the meal, but it became more pained as we ate. I can't remember how he talked Mom into letting him follow us back home. All I knew was that we were under attack.

As I played with my Hot Wheels in the living room, Mom and the friendly man sat in two facing recliners. Mom was adept with others. People always thought she liked them, but most of them were wrong. That night, however, I sensed her panic. When the friendly man stepped out to make a call, she whispered that I should announce in front of him that it was time for my bath, followed by bed. Leave her alone with him?

Minutes later, dumbly splashing in the tub, I didn't know how long to wait. I was terrified of what I might see if I left too soon. Finally, I heard tires screech, a vehicle speeding down our street. Mom slipped inside the bathroom. She tried to breathe, had to try harder. She said I was a good boy. I needed to hear that. Was that man her friend? She insisted I never mention him again. I sat useless in my lukewarm bath.

Louis invites me to watch him penetrate the boy, some flip-tail poof with magenta-streaked hair and clothes one size too snug. His haughty profile pic on the website gives no clue to his eagerness for debasement. I've been stalling in discussing Louis's desire to be raped. I've been refusing his meth; his promises I'll lose my pesky inhibition. I try to watch. The twink glares at me, apparently furious he can't enjoy his degradation without witnesses. Louis doesn't notice me step over the threshold, the bolt clicking when I carefully shut the door.

Louis moans from behind the door, his grunts escalating in pitch. He's about to come. We're definitely not boyfriends, but I feel a spark of accomplishment when I recognize the sound.

The bedroom door bursts open, and I take in Louis, my detestable college-boy ex's own ex. Sweat drenches his dark curls. He hasn't shaved in a couple of days. I want him like a baby wants a tit. The feeling is mutual because Louis throws his arms around me and embarks on a long, perhaps legendary, kiss. He maneuvers me toward the front door, deftly angling me so I can't glance into the twink's bedroom. I hear, however, the faint click of his door. I might love the man sweeping me into the night, but others find that word so elastic. It seems to describe any emotion that doesn't suck.

"It's too bad you didn't stick around." Louis grins. I'm cruising down one of the main drags in Tyler, debating with myself whether he'll want to stay the night.

"I'm glad you got off."

Louis laughs and raps his knuckles against the passenger window. I glance over, struck at how confident and serene he seems in this moment. If he's still disappointed that I haven't raped him, he hides it well. I want to tell him. I want to tell him everything. He feels safe courting his great taboo, in my presence. I owe him the same trust.

"Don't drive so fast, Jared. I'm riding dirty."

"I knew who you were the first time we met."

"No, you didn't. You couldn't remember me the second time we fucked."

I explain my list, my mission to fuck every man that Doug had claimed to love. Yes, he's on the list. Yes, that's why I seduced him. No, that's not why I keep inviting him to Tyler. Finished, I notice a vacuum inside my chest. The secret has grown so immense, its absence announces itself physically. I grip the steering wheel and ease up on the gas. I'm waiting. It's the only thing I hate worse than dreaming.

"What the fuck will it prove?" His noise scrunches in distaste. He looks at me like I haven't bathed in a week. "I'm glad I could help," he says bitterly. "Sometimes I wondered what you and Doug talked about when you were alone." At my complex, Louis hops from my car to his. I ask if he'll return soon.

"I was thinking . . ." I tell him. It's never easy to lie. You can't predict how a deception will evolve. Tell your best friend she doesn't look fat and she might abandon her family. Tell your mother that you enjoyed the mother/son spa day and six months later you both die in a horrible crash while heading to that same spa. "If you wanted to do what . . ." I say. "You know, what you said you like. If you wanna do that next time, I think we can."

Louis's eyes dim. The radio, a tinny trickle from the speakers, offers crude ambiance for whatever must happen next. Louis shuts off the engine and smacks his skull against the headrest. "Don't worry about that rape shit," he says. "It's not fun unless you really want to hurt me." Holding hands, we cross the lot to my apartment.

Jordan looked nothing like his profile pic. It occurred to me, as he drove us to the supermarket, that the photo had been angled in a way that flattered and slimmed. Yes, Jordan was fat. He was short. He was short and fat. Mortified, I followed him through the store, lagging so far behind that my blind date hollered for me to catch up. He walked with his hands held up, as if a purse hung from the crook of his elbow. His hips twitched. His eyes rolled. He was a parody of an effeminate man doing a parody of an effeminate man. I was in the midst of another doomed bid for sobriety.

The food resting in my lap, Jordan driving us to his place, I made it clear I was looking for a platonic relationship. Fortunately, he didn't ask when I'd arrived at this decision. He made a salad of thick noodles and cold shrimp. He talked about himself, asked about me, and then cut me off to talk more about himself. He dropped hints that I shouldn't expect him to bottom. I was too horrified to respond.

Maybe Jordan realized, in a moment of clarity, that I was quietly plotting an escape. He confided, hushed tone, and bowed head, that he'd been raped twice. He was indignant but made sure I understood that he'd put that behind him. "I'm a firm believer in sexual karma," he announced. I didn't tell him I was sorry.

After a stretched silence, he asked for my thoughts. I checked my watch and insisted, through a forced grin, that I must get home. My dealer had promised to text. After he dropped me off, after insisting we embrace, I lied awake in bed, unspeakably angry. It was the most audacious guilt trip I'd ever taken. It should've been recorded for posterity. I wondered if his rapists ever discussed him on their first dates.

—◁∿▷—

The door to Louis's bedroom is ajar. I place my ear at the opening, puzzled to hear scratching against metal. The door flies open, Louis standing before me. He looks pale and emptied, like a milk jug drained of its last drop. His eyelids flutter as he takes me in.

"I called from the road," I say. "You didn't answer."

"Sorry. I got busy with Peppermint."

"Who's Peppermint?" I think I know the answer.

He smiles and ushers me in, the whole room filling with rattles and squeaks. Stacked atop one another in the corners, on shelves, and even under his bed, are hamster cages. The rodents run in their wheels. A few suck at their eyedropper-sized water bottles. His bedroom hums with the futile energy of a top spinning beyond a child's reach. So goddamn many of them.

"I didn't know you liked animals."

"Not all animals: just these." He opens the sock drawer and plucks a bag of crystals from inside. "They don't live very long, you know." He pulverizes a couple of crystals beneath his driver's license. "I'll have to bury every last one. It's bittersweet."

I nod and ease myself onto the bed. Louis wears only a sagging pair of gym shorts and a Nike t-shirt. He's barefoot. His feet thump against the cement floor as he moves about the room. I don't know if we'll have sex after I drove here from Tyler. There are so many variables. All I want to know now, however, is why his bedroom has no carpet.

"The hamsters kept wetting it. After a while, I couldn't get rid of the stink."

"But they're in cages?"

"I like to let them roam," he says.

"Can you cut me a line of that?"

I've seen his small and dingy world, and unless I'm willing to dash back to my car right now, I need something to blunt the impact. I kiss him, gently, lips staying closed. In fables, the princess wakes and marries whatever dude kisses her, out of gratitude. After I kiss Louis, he hands me a clipped section from a straw. The dope jets inside my nostril, the bitterness budding at the back of my throat. After that line, I return to the bed, wanting to be alone with my high. I recall why I stopped this shit: I don't have to worry whether it loves me back.

No, wait. That's why I started again.

Sprawled on the bed, I don't notice how much dope he does or how quickly it disappears. I catch a glimpse of him, though, returning the empty baggie to his sock drawer. Tweaked, the scratching against the cages sounds like children eating popcorn. He asks if I want a *Playgirl*, but muscle magazines are so cut-and-paste cheap, at least compared to their girlie counterparts. I want to cry, high or sober, when I open one.

Louis lies on his front, propped up on his elbows, leafing through the pictures of oiled, leering studs. It takes a moment before I notice his hips are moving to the same metronome rhythm he employs when we fuck. One of his hands is tucked beneath his abdomen, presumably yanking on his cock. The precision with which his hips and hands are timed perversely impresses me. Surely, though, the cold concrete floor is complicating things. His bare ass, gym shorts tugged to his upper thighs, bobs up and down. I don't have a magazine and I've resisted pawing my crotch, but I'm still getting hard. I want to violate Louis in front of his hamster harem. I wonder if his agonized cries would spur the rodents to run faster in their wheels.

Louis hasn't looked at me once since taking to the floor. I tell him I have to piss. Once out of his bedroom, I dash toward the front door. I could've raped him. He likes it, and I might have liked it. After we were done, though, what next? Our business would be finished. I've landed all but one of Doug's exes, and the last is sadly too far away to pursue.

If I ever rape Louis, I'll want Doug to know.

In the driveway, I start the car and turn to look over the seat. On the trunk's lid, a beige-striped hamster licks its paws clean. In a crazed moment, I consider taking him home. I kill the engine, trying to think. My erection betrays me, my sad delusion that I'm a decent man. Fuck the restraining order.

I call Doug. He answers on the second ring.

—◦∿∿◦—

Avery, believe it or not, hooked up with other guys. A few weeks before, at the club, I'd discovered him in the men's room stall. He never hooked up with me, though. I made myself available in the only ways I knew: I strutted beside him while he took vodka shots, chatted with him online while using a more attractive man's profile pic, coaxed one of his drunken exes to reveal what moves turned his crank. Zilch.

I went to an after party three years ago. I did bumps with a couple of friends, in the bathroom, while our host held court downstairs. After we were done, after these friends refused to suck me off, they headed downstairs without me. I tried doorknobs. The furthest one on the right swung open at my touch.

Avery snored softly atop a twin bed with a floral bedspread and hot-pink canopy. He was gorgeous, lithe, pouty-lipped, and long-limbed. He reminded me of a guy I knew during junior high who lathered himself more slowly whenever I stared. Standing at the side of bed, I watched his eyeballs twitter beneath their lids. It wasn't done consciously, but my trembling hand passed over his chest, pressing more firmly as it traveled toward his crotch. Avery snorted and rolled over, his back now to me.

I should go, I told myself. Instead, I crawled beside him, moving too delicately to disturb the bedsprings, and then laid on my side, facing him. I kissed him, keeping my lips closed. He tasted like peppermint. He mumbled for me to stop but never fully woke. He rolled over onto his back, grunting, and I maneuvered my thin body on top of his. No one denied Jared Glidewell!

I kissed him harder and rubbed my hips against his. He snapped awake. "Gross," he cried, roughly wiping his mouth with the back of his hand. I retreated to the other side of the bed. He swung his legs off the bed to stand, but his feet betrayed him. His face smacked the edge of the nightstand, his body hitting the floor.

My breath solidified inside my lungs. Avery sprawled, again unconscious, on the floor. A gash on his forehead wept blood. I dashed downstairs, relieved no one noticed. Two weeks later, I learned that he'd survived. I'd left him, though, with a humbling scar. I watched him, stringing along the buffest guy in the club, slip into a men's room stall.

I stopped snorting. I lasted three years. My mother and Lucille, they were so proud.

—◦〰◦—

The rent-a-cop insists we order food if we plan to stay at Whataburger, not far from his parents' home. It's weekend visit. I huddle over my small fries, desperate to make this encounter last, and Doug plops down across from me, apple pie in hand. He mumbles, at a volume the rent-a-cop surely hears, about how safe and protected he feels.

My eyes pop. "Baby, cut it out. He might call the real police."

"Don't call me that, Jared."

"What?"

"I'm not your baby," he says.

I nod meekly. My gaze skips about the room. I've imagined so many long, languorous conversations with him that it shames me how nothing comes to mind, forcing an awkward silence between us. Finally, I ask him how his latest show went. He studies theater at a university in north Texas.

His face darkens. "How do you know what show I was in?"

Panicked, I spit out something about hearing a rumor. In reality, I Google his name at least once a week. I found online articles reporting his high-school activities. It shocks me how well he did in debate.

"What bullshit," he says. "By the way, I know about the list."

After Doug suggested we meet here, during our phone conversation after I'd left Louis with his hamsters and muscle magazine, I promised myself I'd come clean. As for the rest, I don't see how Doug knowing could help my cause. Now, however, I sit exposed across a grimy Formica table. I'm a freak. This is stupid. I've been hoping that once I reveal my master plan to Doug, he will understand the depth of my devastation and realize that such agony exists only in the presence of true love. But now that another has exposed me, I sound deranged.

"I called Louis after I hung up with you," he says, tone flat. "I wanted to check on him. He loses the thread sometimes."

"He was pissed when I left. That's why—"

Doug simply raises his hand as if taking an oath. "Let's end this, Jared." The rent-a-cop's cheeks flush bright red as Doug describes what he'll do for me if I vanish forever. Louis is done with me, too, he adds. I accept his terms. I must— my fries are gone.

From the back seat of my Sentra, I glance over my shoulder to make sure the rent-a-cop stays inside. Doug, crammed back there with me, yanks my sweatpants down to my knees. He doesn't have a condom but assures me I'm safe, and he has no intention of spurting inside me. Our position makes it impossible to look at his face. That's okay. I don't want the Doug kneeling behind me to overwhelm the Doug locked safely in my fantasies. He's let his dark-blond hair get shaggy, and still can't manage a close shave. When combined with his rugged physique, he looks like a rugby player. He's a wonder and a miracle.

I'm more surprised than he is when I smack his temple.

"What the hell, dude? You want me to lose my hard-on?"

"Get the fuck out." I tremble and sweat. It's like indigestion. "I am *done* with you!" Once he steps on the asphalt, he warns, our deal is off. I flail before him, blindly slapping his face and chest. He doesn't defend himself. Still, I can't stop, my violence the only evidence that I exist.

Minutes later, I'm back on the highway, headed to Tyler. I said no to Doug, my college-boy bastard ex. I would've liked it. I used to like everything Doug did to me. It's a simple equation: He was the one doing it, handling me with those huge, hard hands.

I'm driving too fast now. My bed feels too wide when I sleep alone. Most nights I sack out on the couch before cooking show reruns. I'm an attractive man—not like Doug, but I can still click on the charisma. I have options. Abruptly, tires screeching, I switch lanes. I've always had better luck in Longview. Surely I'll see some men I know, men I don't.

⊸⥈ LOVE IS ALL THERE IS ⥈⊸

Peter H Denton

MAURITIUS, SOUTH INDIAN OCEAN

Kristen had killed her husband without forethought. A spat had cascaded into a catastrophe. Windhover, their seventy-foot high-tech catamaran, lay anchored in the open roadstead in the capital of the Solomon Islands, Honiara.

Mel jumped into the cockpit where Kristen was reading *The Poisonwood Bible*.

Mel said, "Would you please come and man the safety line? I need to replace the VHF antenna."

The tall mast had steps along its length all the way to the top. Kristen's job was to pay out the safety line as Mel ascended and keep it snug as he descended.

Kristen asked, "Why do you need to do it in the middle of the day? Why not wait until it gets cooler? I'm simply not coming out onto the deck until the sun is lower."

Mel didn't answer. He returned to the deck, strapped on his tool belt, and started up the mast. The ninety-foot mast had a spreader that held the support cables away from the mast in order to stabilize them. The spreader was a flat, six-inch-wide piece of aluminum that extended out three feet from the mast. While at anchor, a bird had built a nest on the top of the spreader. As Mel reached the level of the spreader, the startled bird shrieked and clawed Mel's face. He fell backward and dropped with the single, short dull thud of a fallen bag of rice.

Kristen understood instantly.

She was tormented by guilt. He'd be alive if she hadn't sat like a lump in the cockpit and refused to help him. Everyone told her the grief would pass or at least slowly lessen. It hadn't.

She awoke one morning in Mauritius, far-flung in an ocean where every island is far-flung, and it was over. Mel had come to her in a dream and ordered her to begin living. Kristen emerged into the cockpit, hungry for the cook's breakfast of pineapple, mango, and papaya laced with lime.

She said to her crew, "I promised you the Seychelles and the Maldives. I can't keep my promise. I have to return to my family in Australia. It's that simple."

None of her crew desired a trip through the Roaring Forties to Australia. They began packing. Kristen walked to the marina office and posted an ad for a new crew.

She went below and opened a drawer that hadn't been opened for years. The drawer contained a plain black but silky dress. Earrings. Pantyhose. Cosmetics. Even out of practice, after an hour, her image pleased. She brushed the tangles out of her long, thick, curly black hair. Kristen put money in her purse, locked the boat, and walked up the cobblestone streets to the Hyatt-Regency. She was unsure what to order in the restaurant but knew for damn sure it wasn't going to be fish.

She ate slowly. For too long, food had been a need, not a pleasure. After eating and giving the waiter an extravagant tip, she went into the lounge, sat in a plush chair in front of a table carved of precious hardwood, and ordered Courvoisier and coffee, black.

A young woman with short, carefully styled hair approached the table and said, "You look like you could use some company."

Kristen smiled up at her and said, "I'd be delighted."

The fine-boned woman, dressed elegantly said, in an equally elegant French accent, "I'm Helene Grimaud, and I have the honor of speaking to?"

"Kristen with a K, Carson with a C."

Before Kristen had left the boat, she had removed her wedding ring, put it in a drawstring satin pouch, and placed the pouch in the back of the drawer. Without thinking, she had given Helene her maiden name.

From the first, they spoke as if they were old friends.

That night, they didn't talk for long. Kristen told Helene where Windhover was berthed and invited her to join her there for lunch. Helene agreed with the provision that she, Helene, would bring the food.

At noon precisely, Helene asked for permission to come aboard. Kristen laughed and said, "You have permission, but in the future, just step aboard."

Kristen loved looking at Helene, who glowed with an aura as subtle and sexy as Chanel Number Five. Kristen felt a tidal tug toward her and understood that it was that very force that drew a man toward a woman. How silly of her to react this way to Helene. But then, for so long there had been so little perfume in her life. Human contact did not require touch. Simple friendship was a thrill. Kristen stood up and rushed below, saying, "There's something I must show you."

She returned to the deck with a picture of Mel and her. "Your Mel, he is magnifique. Look at the muscles. Un vrai homme. And you, so tall, so proud, with your face blushed with the cosmetic of love."

Kristen dropped to the cushioned seat and sobbed as if drowning. Helene embraced her and said, "Ma cheri, I'm so sorry. I did not mean to unearth your pain."

Kristen slowed down and regained composure. "No, Helene, it's not that. Not tears of sorrow. I have cried the last of those. Tears of celebration, of remembrance, of the joy I had feared was lost. I am delighted to share them."

After the light lunch, Kristen asked Helene about herself. "I'm an ornithologist."

Kristen laughed. "That's not possible. You are so chic."

"And you are so very antipodean. Every woman must look her best. I not only study birds; I also love them. Two weeks ago, I was a thousand miles south, on Iles Amsterdam, an ugly rotten tooth of an island, but a paradise of birds. I was forced to quit."

"Forced? By who?"

"Men. Who else? I was one woman among thirty-eight men, most of them Frenchmen."

"Australian men would be just as bad."

"I doubt that."

Kristen walked Helene back to the Hilton and said, "Windhover is a spacious, gracious lady. I have so much room. Let me be your hotel."

"Merci."

The new, fondly found friends spent the week sailing to the jungled coves hidden on the coast of Mauritius. Windhover was a snap to sail, and Helene quickly took to sailing. They returned to port and on Sunday, veiled, took the Sacrament in the Basilica de Port-Louis.

As they walked down the steps, Kristen stopped and said, "Come with me to Australia."

"Bon. When do we set sail, Mon Capitaine?"

For a week, they prepared the boat for the long, hard passage ahead. Helene convinced Kristen that they should stop at Ile Amsterdam to look at the birds.

Ile Amsterdam appeared first as a gray cloud on the horizon and rose out of the water like a slowly breaching whale. The two women stood at the wheel and cheered. Kristen trusted her navigation, but after two weeks on the limitless ocean, she had begun to doubt the existence of land.

The scientists at the research station were happy to welcome Helene back, particularly with her statuesque Aussie captain. Kristen and Helene decided to stay for a few days. They had agreed that the trip to Ile Amsterdam would be a trial run to see if they remained amiable. They had.

Helene led Kristen on a short expedition up over the active volcano on the southwest end of the island and down a steep slope to the albatross rookeries. Kristen, as every sailor, knew the albatross, whose wingspread exceeds that of any other living bird, but she had never seen the tiny baby balls of fluff, protected by a mother who would exact swift justice on anyone who imperiled her children.

Kristen wiped away a tear at the sight of such a splendid work of God, wrought by the magic of evolution. She hugged Helene, who understood.

The trial was over. Helene was on board.

Before their departure from Ile Amsterdam, Kristen reviewed Windhover's unique safety features, which included waterproof hatches that, as on a naval vessel, could isolate sections of the hull. At dawn Kristen warmed up the Yanmar diesels, went forward, engaged the winch, and raised the anchor. The sails could be adjusted with a bank of lines and winches installed in the safety of the cockpit, so it was easy to handle Windhover even in a gale.

Kristen and Helene were not alone. Cruising had created a safety net. Ben, an American Air Force sergeant stationed at the SAC base on Diego, came up on an amateur band every day at 1600 hours. Somebody always knew Windhover's position.

Windhover had an autopilot, but that robot did not lessen the importance of keeping a watch. Kristen worried about collisions with logs, whales, or cargo containers, fallen from freighters, that floated just beneath the surface.

During the day, Helene and Kristen shared the watch in the protected cockpit. They took turns in an agreeable, random fashion. Every few minutes one of them stood and surveyed the curve of the horizon. At night, if they saw ships' lights or heard the ominous thrum of a giant diesel, they ducked below to the radar and changed course if needed.

The sea simplifies life and reduces it to its basic elements. Waves swam next to them, and birds skipped from white top to white top. Albatross often hung above the stern for hours, suddenly dipped into the sea, and surfaced proudly with unfortunate fish in their beaks. Sunlight rarely peeked through the clouds, but when it did, the world sparkled and myriad tiny rainbows kissed the tips of white tops. The albatross blazed white, and Windhover shimmered in an electric aura. Time dissolved and was compressed into an endless moment. The *now* was sufficient. In decent weather.

At 1600 hours she dialed into Ben's net and listen to the weather report. A disturbance in the Arafura Sea was developing. "All vessels to the west, on or about fifteen degrees south, should seek protection."

Helene asked, "Any news?"

"Yes. A hurricane is brewing near Darwin."

Helene said, "That must be at least a thousand miles away."

"Actually two thousand miles and heading west.

Helene said, "Sounds like bad news for somebody, but not us."

Kristen said, "But."

"But what?"

"A hurricane sends out waves in every direction like a pebble in a pond. The pond is the Indian Ocean and the pebble is the size of Mount Everest. The waves travel as fast as a freight train. At the moment, the bulk of Australia blocks the waves, but once the storm has passed Australia, the swells could hit in a day. Two at most."

After the evening meal Kristen said, "I'm so glad you're here. Men can be such a nuisance."

Helene replied, "I have lost interest in men. The only time I enjoy sex is when it's recreation and I can go home to my own bed, to my own life."

"Since Mel, I have been sexless. But even before he died, sex was like crème brulé. A treat when served fresh, but otherwise out of mind."

An explosive burst sent them from their seats. Kristen stood and ran to the port. A foot below the surface, a red slab, an almost sunken cargo container, coursed past. Kristen grabbed the helm and hollered to Helene to reef the main.

A red light flashed and a buzzer on the console screamed. "We're taking on water in the starboard hull. Go below. Check the watertight hatches."

Helene yelled, "She's dogged down tight, but water is gushing out the bottom"

"The collision warped the bulkhead."

Kristen moved with the silent assuredness of a surgeon clamping off a vein, ran forward, held onto the forestay, and swung out beyond the hull. She returned to the cockpit. "Hole the size of your fist." She held a six-by-six tarp. "We'll go forward and slip it like a sleeve over the bow, pull it tight, and tie it off. Won't stop all the water but enough so we can pump out the compartment and cover the hole with plywood."

Windhover drifted in the wind. Using lines attached to the corners of the canvas, Kristen and Helene tried to slip the tarp around the front of the bow. The waves slapped the tarp aside. The boat had steadied, but each needed a hand to hold on. Two hands were not enough to guide the tarp into place. Kristen stood on the bow and hung out over the water. Helene stood facing her on the mesh trapeze that extended between the two hulls of the catamaran. They kept trying to lasso the hull but again and again failed. Helene flopped down onto the trapeze and dug her feet into the mesh. She then had two hands and a more secure position. Three hands worked the canvas into place.

They raced below to the waterproof bulkhead. The tarp had slowed the flow enough so that the emergency bilge pump could take over. Kristen motioned Helene to hold a precut piece of plywood against the hole. Water pushed the plywood back. Helene sat down and with both feet held the plywood in place. Kristen secured it with a cordless drill.

At 1800 hours Kristen and Helene hovered over the radio. Ben repeatedly announced, "Hurricane Chakra is at category three. Urgent. All vessels, in possible storm tracks, steam to safe haven. Eye located three hundred miles northeast of Land's End, Australia."

Kristen heard the message. For now Australia blocked the waves, but Chakra would soon send killer waves their way.

The barometer was falling. A local storm was brewing. Double trouble.

During the night, the true wind increased to forty-five but steady from the west. Windhover was running away from the wind, so if she stopped, she would be hit by its full force. Speed was a constant danger. If the bow pierced the face of a big wave, the yacht would stop short and tumble over.

In the Timor Sea due north of Australia, hurricane Chakra was making slow progress to the west. As long as Australia stood between Chakra and Windhover, she was protected.

At times, Windhover pegged out at twenty knots and never slowed below fifteen. Four hundred miles a day. Kristen yelled, "Wowee, zowee!"

Helene yelled back, "Zowee, wowee!"

What a rush to climb to the top of a twenty-five-foot wave and surf down it on a seventy-foot-long surfboard.

The clouds darkened, and when the sun set, the only light was the phosphorescence glowing from the bow waves. At night, the thrills became fears. The wind rose and continued to rise. Nasty wind waves began to form. Windhover skidded occasionally into a large, solitary wave and stalled but recovered quickly. An extended stall would blow out the sails, but worse could flip the big boat head over heels. Kristen and Helene lowered the sail. Kristen couldn't slow the boat. The mast and hull alone pushed Windhover forward at twenty knots.

Kristen said, "Time to stream out warps." It sounded simple, but in the violent wind and the unceasing movement of the boat, nothing was easy. Like climbing the face of a mountain cliff, each movement needed planning and every action carefully considered. If one of them fell overboard, she would never see dry land again.

Kristen tied one end of a thick, six-hundred-foot-long rope to the jib winch, and Helene tied the other end to a large cleat. They paid out the line until it doubled and formed a loop. As soon as the rope was fully stretched out, the boat slowed to seven knots. The loops of rope hanging astern not only slowed the boat but also acted like the tail of a kite and kept Windhover facing downwind.

The noise was horrible. The wind roared off the waves and set the rigging ringing like a claxon. The waves beat the hull in a ragged rhythm from which there was no escape. Even shouting into each other's ears, they could scarcely hear each other.

Kristen said, "If the wind continues to build, the top of the waves will begin to break. "

"What can we do about it?"

Kristen replied, "Shut off the autopilot and start steering. An hour on. An hour off. When you're not on the wheel, go below and make some sandwiches and a couple of thermoses of coffee. The waterproof hatch to the main cabin has to be dogged down. Sooner or later, a breaking wave is going to Niagara over us and fill the cockpit."

Kristen had the instincts of a Sydney surfer, and Helene was learning fast. Each of them, when it was her turn to steer, guided the boat down the face of the waves at twenty degrees short of straight ahead. The waves were so high that when the boat dipped into the trough, the waves behind blocked the wind and they slowed down dangerously. Like bicycling down a hill, they needed to pedal hard to get up to speed on the slope rising directly ahead.

A catamaran can never be flipped unless it turns sideways and the wind catches the bottom of the hull. Sailors call this disastrous situation a broach. Each time Windhover slid down the face of a wave, the helmsman had to maneuver to keep the boat facing forward to avoid a broach. The turbulent water battered the rudders and at times, the steering wheel could not be turned. At other times, when the stern lifted out of the water, the wheel spun out of control.

Kristen calculated when Chakra's waves would arrive. They were surfing on waves thirty feet high. Perhaps Chakra's spinoff would make little difference.

Nighttime was a nightmare. Steering required intense concentration, which kept fear at bay, but off the wheel there was time enough for terror. Kristen had studied accounts of sailing in the Southern Ocean, because study was the only form of preparation.

Stronger winds transferred more kinetic energy into the waves, which were already at the limit. Like surf breaking on a beach, massive waves crumbled into frothy cascades along a thousand-foot stretch. Windhover floated over the foam with never a wipeout. So far.

Kristen heard a rumbling roaring above the rest and looked behind her to see a fang of breaking wave poised to impale Windhover. Kristen and Helene were harnessed to the deck, and when that wave broke, the lifelines stopped them from being swept overboard. Or they should have. Kristen was at the wheel and hung onto it. She looked behind her. Helene was gone.

Kristen gagged with panic but reflexively initiated the established protocol: She punched the man overboard button (MOB), which displayed the boat's exact position on the GPS, turned on the deck lights, reefed the main, dropped the jib, and fired up the diesels. Conscious or not, Helene's lifejacket would keep her head above water and activate a strobe light. Kristen scrutinized the ocean around her but saw nothing. In three minutes, Windhover had traveled half a mile. Guided by the GPS, Kristen steered the boat back to the MOB position. In the fierce headwinds, the diesels just barely moved Windhover forward.

In that instant Kristen realized who Helene was to her.

She locked the wheel, grabbed the binoculars, and raced forward to look for the strobe. Helene could be on any side the boat. Kristen picked her way around the boat's perimeter, careful to keep her footing and to work her lifeline around the obstacles on the deck. Spray clouded the binoculars. Kristen searched with unaided eyes. When she reached the stern, she saw the strobe light not twenty feet away, and moving. Closer!

Coagulated dread seized her, and she ran to shut off the engines. Helene had never left the boat. Her lifeline had snagged the rudder and now was caught in the propeller, which was dragging her forward to a bloody death. Helene spiraled like a hooked fish. Her head bobbed at the surface, but she might already be dead.

Helene was caught in the starboard prop. Kristen turned the wheel hard to starboard, which brought Helene to the side of the boat. Kristen picked up the end of the jib line and dropped it to Helene, four feet beneath her. Helene grabbed the rope. Many overboards died dangling from the side of the boat because their hapless rescuers couldn't pull them aboard. But Kristen thought she could.

She reached down with a boat hook and pulled back the rope, which Helene had strung through her lifeline harness. Kristen pulled Helene's sodden weight, but the battering waves thwarted her. She cleated off the line and left Helene, who cried out in terror. Kristen had already dropped the main and pulled the boom above Helene's head. She ran the rope tied to Helene through a pulley on the boom and wound it around a winch. She turned the winch handle inch by inch, and Helene rose from the water like the corpse she almost had become. Kristen swung the boom back aboard and lowered Helene onto the deck.

She sped to the console, reset the sails, returned to Helene, carried her below, and laid her on a bunk. She undressed her friend with care. Kristen dried Helene's delicate body with a towel. Since the day they met, another storm had been brewing. For a moment, the pounding of her heart silenced the maelstrom outside. Kristen gazed at Helene's tiny breasts and fleecy triangle and was pierced by desire. Kristen quickly redressed Helene in warm clothes.

Helene said, "I'm sorry; I'm so sorry. You risked the boat; you risked your life. Merci; merci. Je t'aime; je t'aime."

Kristen reached beneath Helene, lifted her light body to her, and squeezed. "I love you back."

And she ran to the deck to face the storm.

The ocean increasingly lost its shape and was nearly impossible to judge up from down. Chakra had arrived. The sea had degenerated into chaos. The regiments of swells were breaking up into pyramids that collapsed and rose up again. Windhover thrashed about so hard that the two women could only move by crawling. Kristen said, "If we don't do something before last light, we'll be dead by morning."

Spume as hard as hail spat off the tops of the waves. Not all the water running down Helene's face came from the waves. She said, "Just tell me what to do."

"You're not going to like it," Kristen admitted.

"Merde, who cares what I like?"

Kristen lashed the wheel. "Let's go below." She looked astern, and when the coast was clear, she undogged the watertight hatch and ducked inside, with Helene close behind her. "I want to sink the boat."

"So that we can end our suffering?" Helene asked.

"No; to save us. The sink and toilet drains have stopcocks so that in bad weather, water can't flow into the boat. I'm going to open all the stopcock valves and leave them open until each hull is almost full of water. Ten cubic meters of water in each hull is ten tons of water. We'll sink three feet. We'll outsmart the ocean. With Windhover floating just below the surface, the waves will lose their power to hurt us."

"How can you know what will happen?"

"I don't know anything. If my strategy doesn't work, we're dead."

The hull filled quickly. Windhover sank to the sea's surface, and water sloshed across the deck. Only the mast and the main cabin stuck out of the turbulent ocean. Sometimes Windhover submerged and only the mast stood above the seas. The watertight bulkheads held.

Kristen sent out an SOS. Sooner than expected she heard Ben and said to him, "Your voice is music."

Ben replied, "I'll keep this wavelength open and ask headquarters to try to scare up a vessel near you."

A rescue could be as dangerous as the sea itself. No helicopter could possibly fly in these conditions, and a large boat, pounded by the same waves that beset her, could crush Windhover. Kristen's only hope was to drift closer to Australia and be picked up by an Australian Navy helicopter when the wind dropped.

Waves swept over the deck, crashed, and sometimes broke on top of it. The momentum of the shocks threw the women against the bulkheads. Kristen, grasping for handholds, crawled along the cabin floor to a locker and pulled out two bright-orange survival suits. They struggled into them. The suits were thick and spongy and prevented further bruising. They were roasting and clumsy, but who cared.

The radio was of no use, so Kristen screwed down its waterproof cover. They pulled the seat cushions underneath the galley table and wedged themselves between them. Kristen tried to talk to Helene, but Helene had temporarily left her body. Soon after, Kristen found herself floating in a soft supportive sea of dreams.

Windhover gently rocked her awake. She peeled off her survival suit and checked on Helene, who opened her eyes and was smiling. Kristen rushed to the SSB radio and removed the waterproof cover. A stream of water poured out. Books were reduced to pulp, clothing floated in unrecognizable tangles, and a bottle of ketchup bobbed on the water's surface like a red channel buoy.

Kristen cried for her wounded Windhover. She cried for her arrogance. She cried an altogether different stream of tears for her courage, her life, and the gift of Helene.

She undogged the hatch and stepped out into the cockpit. The wind was down to twenty. A few inches of water sloshed across the deck. A small spark of pride glowed in her chest as she looked around for damage. She had a mast, and that was all she really needed. She grasped the wheel and turned it slowly and then more quickly. It turned, but much too easily. The rudders were gone.

Helene emerged, ran to her, and hugged her with healthy strength. They held hands in silence. Kristen said, "Enough of this girly bullshit. Was Ahab weepy at the end of a terrible storm?"

Helene knew these tough words meant nothing. Things had changed and long since had been changed. The fluffy baby albatrosses had welded their spirits. Whatever time God granted was theirs forever.

"No. I'm sure Ahab wouldn't have been weepy, but we're just girls. Girls can weep whenever we want to. What are your orders, Mon Capitan?"

"The electronics are dead. I have the waterproof hand-held VHF, but it's only good for twenty miles."

Kristen didn't say it, but thought *I don't want to be rescued. Windhover has brought us this far, and I'm going to bring her home to port. She has saved our lives, and I'm going to save hers.*

Helene asked, "How far is Australia?"

"Three to five hundred miles. Punch on the diesels." A groan from each engine. Then nothing.

"That's no big surprise. The batteries are cracked or short-circuited. The rudders are gone. Australia is somewhere to the north and somewhere to the east. If we sail to the northeast, we will bump into her somewhere. We have the three essentials: a mast, sails, and a compass. Oh, yes. The fourth essential: two live sailors."

Helene said, "And cinque: Ben knows were out here. But how about all the water in the hulls?"

"I told you we're going to Australia; I didn't say how fast."

Sailing Windhover without a rudder was not as difficult as Kristen had anticipated. With the wind steady from the west, Kristen and Helene were able to set the sails on a compass course without much adjustment. On the fifth day after the storm had ended, they reached the northern limits of the westerlies.

On the seventh day a plane flew by overhead. They shot off two of their precious flares. The plane waggled its wings. Kristen answered on the VHF, "What is your position?"

"Two hundred and eighty miles to the southeast of Perth. Do you copy?"

"I copy," she answered.

"Hold tight. We'll have a 'copter there by the morning."

Helene was overjoyed, but Kristen wasn't. A helicopter could rescue them, but it couldn't rescue Windhover.

The Australian helicopter showed up at nine the next morning. It hovered and lowered a man down to the deck.

"You go first, Helene. I need to make a few last checks."

Helene hugged her.

Over the radio the pilot said, "Hold on tight. We'll be back down to rescue you."

"Negative on that transmission. I'm not going down with the boat, but I'm not leaving her, either," Kristen said.

"This is Captain Forsyth. I am ordering you to be off-lifted."

"With all due respect Captain Forsyth, fuck off."

The winds blew fair, and the winds blew foul. Kristen knew where she was and where she was going. It didn't matter how long it took. She closed on Perth, and small boats sailed out to greet her. She was not offered a tow or food because her countrymen had far too much respect to interfere with her heroic solo. The crowd that gathered on the breakwater cheered her on to the dock, where she threw the mooring line to Helene, who helped her off the half-sunken boat. They embraced and cried like babies.

An ambulance stood by and despite her reluctance, she was taken to the Royal Perth Hospital. Helene came to her bedside with a big bouquet of flowers and a box of Belgian chocolates. They hugged.

"What's next, Mon Capitan?"

Kristen grabbed Helene's hand, "Ma cheri, know this. You'd not have drowned alone. I would've jumped overboard and we'd have drowned together. My past is in the past. You are my future."

Helene leaned over, kissed her, and whispered, "It's you and me, cheri."

Kristen kissed her back. "You are so right. Just you and me, babe."

CONTRIBUTORS

PETER H. DENTON lives and writes in North Carolina. He spent fifteen years during which time he built his gaff rigged cutter, Endurance, and sailed it to the South Pacific. He led scientific expeditions in the area known as Melanesia, i.e. New Guinea, the Solomon Islands, New Caledonia, and the New Hebrides. Much of his writing is based on experiences he had while sailing in, what is correctly called, paradise. Endurance was destroyed in a tropical hurricane and he returned to the United States where he earned a PhD in molecular genetics. His has published three short stories and won an HOnorable mention in the Hemingway short story contest. He has written two novels and is currently working on a memoir about his early years at Harvard University during the psychedelic revolution as well as his years in the New Left, and his adventures in the South Pacific.

ELIZABETH ANN DOMINO was born and raised in Bryan, Texas. She says she is probably the only Mexican who doesn't know how to speak Spanish. Along with her husband, she is raising a blended family of four kids while working a legitimate 9–5 job and serving as Vice President and Press Director for the Houston Writers Guild. A former staff writer for the lifestyle magazine Act Badd, her writing has also been featured in an on-campus publication, *The Bayou Review*, on the blog, *Curators of Dopeness*, as well as her own blog *Ramblings of an Ovary*. She will appear in the 2016 *Listen To Your Mother SouthEast Texas* production this April. Elizabeth started writing in college. She enrolled in a Creative Writing class in Fall of 2007, attending for the sake of fulfilling a requisite for an English credit for her Art degree. She found that writing opened her heart and she became addicted to writing. She attended workshops and joined critique groups. She started out writing dark ironic fiction and later transitioned into semi-autobiographical fiction while maintaining a personal blog on the trials and tribulations of mothering, womaning and in general living. About writing, she says, "It's tough, and I don't have the playbook with all the right moves, and I wanted to know if anyone else out there still felt like a failure. Like that 17-year-old awkward girl in Chemistry class who is always off by one misstep."

Born in Kuala Lumpur, Malaysia, BERNARD (FOONG) YOUNG is a writer and designer who has traveled the globe. He received his Master of Design at the Royal College of Art & Design in London, England, while retailing bridal and evening dresses to Liberty of London, Selfridges, Harrods, and Harvey Nichols. Later, he completed his second Master of Art in Theatre Costuming at the University of Hawaii. He served as Hong Kong Polytechnic University's Fashion professor and as Associate Fashion Design/Illustration Professor to the University of Wisconsin, Madison. Now a resident on the Island of Maui, he has assisted charity organizations in their fund raising events with his extravagant fashion and performance presentations. Foong is writing his seven-book autobiography. *A Harem Boy's Saga* series is published by Solstice Publishing and is available in print, audio and E-books internationally, with a film contract secured with an independent producer operating in Hollywood.

COPPER HAYES appreciates her senses. She filters all her experiences through a sieve that finds something exceptional to see, hear, taste, smell or feel. Especially feel. In spite of her eclectic nature, she has gathered a husband who lets her parade around in a crown (until she needs it knocked off for a spell), a houseful of beagles, a best friend who can hear anything, a colorful, comfortable home, a relatively sane extended family and a Mac Air to capture her rather offbeat personality.

THOMAS KEARNES holds an MA in Screenwriting from the Michener Center for Writers at the University of Texas at Austin. His fiction has appeared or will appear in *Berkeley Fiction Review, SmokeLong Quarterly, Gulf Stream Magazine, wigleaf, Per Contra, Spork, Underground Voices, PANK, Word Riot, Sundog Lit, 3 AM Magazine, Adroit Journal* and elsewhere. His work has also appeared in several LGBT venues, including *Educe Journal, Wilde*, the *Best Gay Stories* series and elsewhere. He has been nominated three times for the Pushcart Prize. He is studying to become a drug dependency counselor. He lives in Houston.

PAUL KRUMREI, JR. was born and Raised in Northern Minnesota, a transplant with a love and passion for all things art. Drawing inspiration from romantic periods in history, combining it with modern styles and art forms to create soft and tender works audiences can relate to. Paul studied Fine Arts at the College of Visual Arts in St. Paul, Minnesota shortly before it closed and further enhanced, challenged, and retaught himself everything he knew about art and design. Connection is what he strives for, whether it be creating a design, a custom piece of jewelry, a portrait painting, or perhaps even a social piece simply to convey a visual message about topics he feel strongly on. Even in different mediums, the soft tender expressions always convey the artists love... of love!

ERIKA SMALL, "BlkShp", is an avid lover of words. She believes in the tremendous power of words and chooses to use her writing to put them together in ways that make others think, feel, do, become and in some cases, just be. She is affectionately known to her friends as "The Storyteller", coined for her ability to tell a story so vividly that readers feel as though they are able to become one with her characters. Erika believes she can and is dedicated to changing the world, one book at a time.

DOROTHY TINKER focuses on stories written within worlds of her own creation. She has been writing since she was thirteen, when friendship with another young writer/poet helped her realize the potential for the stories that fill her mind. Currently, Dorothy's interests include reading in general, exploring other cultures, and languages (both her native tongue of English and most others). She utilizes these, and any other knowledge she can, to expand the worlds and stories she creates in the realms of fantasy, horror, and science fiction.

DAVID WELLING is a Houston-based writer, artist, and graphic designer. His lifelong interest in movies (and the places that show them) led to the writing of *Cinema Houston: From Nickelodeon to Megaplex*, which chronicles the history of movie theatres in Texas' largest city. *Cinema Houston* is the recipient of the 2008 Julia Ideson Award from the Friends of the Texas Room, and the Society of Architectural Historians' 2009 Antoinette Forrester Downing Award. He is now writing fiction. His website and blog is davidwelling.com.

About the Houston Writers Guild

THE HOUSTON WRITERS GUILD is a community of writers of all skill levels striving to improve their craft and career through education and camaraderie.

The Guild was founded in 1998 by Roger Paulding with seven participants and has grown to more than 200 active members today. Over its first fifteen years, the Guild sponsored 36 workshops and six 2-day conferences. Roger led the group until 2013, when he passed the reins to Pamela Fagan Hutchins. On September 17, 2014, after a terrific year of leadership, Pamela passed the torch on to Fernanda Brady and Denise Satterfield. Together they are geared up to take HWG to a higher level. Their vision is, with the help of volunteers, to make the Houston Writers Guild a household name in the writing community.

The Guild offers its members workshops/conferences/webinars to learn about their craft and critique groups with excellent participant feedback. It creates opportunities to build careers through networking, as well as, opportunities for author book sales throughout the Greater Houston area and neighboring communities.

Houston Writers Guild
houstonwritersguild.org
P.O.Box 42255
Houston, TX 77242

www.ingramcontent.com/pod-product-compliance
Lightning Source LLC
Chambersburg PA
CBHW050738230626
47052CB00003BA/515